In the Godforsaken Hinterlands

About *In the Godforsaken Hinterlands*
(*Az Isten háta mögött*, 1911)

Zsigmond Móricz's second published novel represents a uniquely Hungarian take on the adultery theme developed in Gustave Flaubert's wildly popular *Madame Bovary* from 1856. Writing half a century later, in 1911, Móricz introduces surprising innovations into his narrative of a bored teacher's wife and her oblivious husband, making *In the Godforsaken Hinterlands* a classic in its own right. The stultifying atmosphere of semi-feudal Hungary finds telling expression in the fictional town of Ilosva where the novel is set.

In the Godforsaken Hinterlands

A Tale of Provincial Hungary

Written as *Az Isten háta mögött*

by Zsigmond Móricz in 1911

Translated from the Hungarian by

Virginia L. Lewis

Az unalom, mondhatni, egyáltalán nem semmi;
gyúlékony anyag, alattomos érzés.

- Noémi Kiss

Contents

Introduction

Emma Bovary, Thérèse Raquin, Anna Karenina, Effi Briest – these famous forebears of the female protagonist in the Hungarian novel *In the Godforsaken Hinterlands* – Mr. Veres' wife – are among the first characters that come to mind when readers think of the theme of adultery in literature. That Mrs. Veres does not come to mind in this context is due to a number of reasons, none of which bears any relation to her worthiness as a literary heroine. Suffice it to say that the literatures of smaller nations such as Hungary, Romania, Poland, and the like have historically struggled to find their place in the limelight monopolized by the output of the more dominant cultures of France, England, Germany, and Russia. This translation of Hungarian author Zsigmond Móricz's (1879-1942) masterful novel *Az Isten háta mögött* from 1911 represents an effort to draw readers' attention to a literary gem that deserves to occupy its rightful place alongside the more famous novels of Flaubert, Zola, Tolstoy, and Fontane.

Móricz, however, was anything but an epigone. *In the Godforsaken Hinterlands* represents a response to the works alluded to above, a response that highlights at once the universal literary possibilities afforded by the treatment of adultery as a recurring theme, and also the peculiar revelations Móricz's engagement of this theme raises in regard to his Hungarian homeland. Adultery has since biblical times been a theme that allows writers and their audiences to explore the conflict between humans' attempts at achieving self-fulfillment in relative freedom on the one hand, and the often burdensome demands placed on individuals, particularly women, by society on the other.[1] The heroines mentioned above saw in their affairs an opportunity, however dangerous, even destructive, to escape the confinement they experienced in their stifling marriages. Yet what happens when even this outlet, the commission of adultery, proves unattainable? And what circumstances would render even this last resort as a means of achieving self-fulfillment impossible to attain? Móricz's remarkably original contribution to adultery as a literary theme rests in the responses to these questions.

In the Godforsaken Hinterlands connects itself with deliberate openness to its renowned predecessors, in particular to Gustave Flaubert's (1821-1880) masterpiece

---

[1] See Horst S. and Ingrid Daemmrich, *Themen und Motive in der Literatur: Ein Handbuch* (Tübingen: Francke Verlag, 1987), p. 104.

Madame Bovary: Mœrs de province, published in 1856. Tellingly, Móricz has one of his characters, the assistant judge (he lacks an individual name) refer to Mrs. Veres' husband as *Bovary úr* or Mr. Bovary – his wife, whose individuality is so suppressed that she lacks a given name, is never directly linked to Emma Bovary. And herein lies Móricz's master stroke: readers cannot escape the temptation to look for parallels between the Hungarian text and that of Flaubert, and what they find instead are a plethora of contrasts and surprises that provide a unique opportunity to explore the stark limitations of middle-class life in semi-feudal Hungary.

Zsigmond Móricz is perhaps most famous for his unforgettable classic *Be Faithful unto Death* (*Légy jó mindhalálig*, 1920), the sensitive portrait of a Debrecen schoolboy, with autobiographical overtones. But his œuvre extends across four decades and is characterized by equal quantities of breadth and depth, ranging from poignant short stories such as "Seven Pennies" ("Hét krajcár," 1908) to panoramic historical novels such as the trilogy *Transylvania* (*Erdély*, 1922-35). *In the Godforsaken Hinterlands* deserves to find its place among the prized novels of the European continent, first as a sample of Zsigmond Móricz's masterful prose output, secondly as an opportunity to experience the frustrating limitations of early twentieth-century life in provincial Hungary, and last but hardly least as a skillful treatment of a literary theme that never loses its appeal, inasmuch as the theme of adultery affords the opportunity to examine the often painful tensions that inform the relationship between the individual and society.

Virginia L. Lewis, Northern State University

I

Mr. Veres, the primary school teacher, wanted to cross over to the other side of the street, but three large peasant wagons were moving across the road in front of him.

"Dammit," he muttered, "why do they have to be in my way? ... But where could my wife have gone off to? Now the poor curate is stuck waiting there."

He twirled his thick black mustache and rubbed his nose, which was noticeably large; whenever it caused him embarrassment, he always said that the ancient Hungarians were all endowed with similarly large, aquiline noses.

"Good luck at the market!" he called out to the last wagon, where Mrs. Maleczki, the bootmaker's wife, was enthroned high atop her great iron chest. The bootmakers were headed for the market and had to depart now, with the onset of dusk, if they were to arrive there at dawn.

The teacher smiled as he gazed after the bootmaker's wife, who was known by all as a hard woman. A buyer didn't leave her cottage without first enduring the seven torments of hell. Once she'd selected a pair of boots for a man and said: "That's perfect for you," he'd better well buy them, otherwise there would be hell to pay. The other bootmakers at the market envied doddering old Maleczki for his gifted wife, as their chest never failed to grow empty, while those of the others returned home just as they'd started off: full of boots. Once home, though, they made peace with their fate, because Mrs. Maleczki drank and argued, so that not even a saint could have gotten along with her, excepting old Maleczki.

The teacher Mr. Veres stood a bit longer, following the wagon with his eyes. It pleased him to know that these locally made Ilosva boots got so far out into the world and, slung across the peasants' shoulders, would end up in many a tiny village along the Sajó River.

Then he crossed the street with small, quick steps and continued along the other side toward the market square.

He removed a Puerto Rican cigar from his pocket and crunched it between his fingers as he walked. Then he fished out a little cigar cutter and used it to snip off the end; with this he noticed that a young colleague was aproaching him who'd come to town strictly as a substitute teacher, for which reason Veres had never felt the need to address him with the familiar "*te*" form.

"Come here, Mr. Bardócz!" he called out to him.

The young colleague was coming toward him in any case and couldn't have avoided meeting him if he'd wanted to, thus it struck him as pointless that Veres flagged him down "in front of the eyes of the entire town." After all, he wasn't even his supervisor; Pál Veres was only the titulary headmaster of the primary school, so what gave him the right to treat a man like a dog? Waving at him! "Psst!" ... Who does he think he is?

"Haven't you got a match, dear colleague?" Veres asked simply.

"Perhaps ..." And the young man took a box of matches from his pocket and lit one. He held it up to his colleague's cigar, then made to leave without a word.

"See here, see here! Why don't you buy this sort of thing?" Pál Veres said, taking a small nickel object from his pocket; he pressed a little button, the lid sprang open, and in that moment a small yellow flame leapt forth from the object. "What do you say to that?" he asked in satisfaction, and with great delight repeated the feat. He pressed on the lid and it sprang open. "An automatic lighter."

The young teacher smiled in disdain. The whole thing struck him as childish, and anyhow he'd already seen that kind of thing before.

"Right," said Mr. Veres like someone who suddenly has an idea, and with his left hand he grabbed the topmost button on his colleague's coat. But in that moment he noticed that Mrs. Piacsek was standing across the way in the door of the hardware store, and he greeted her:

"I kiss your hand!" He spoke the greeting softly – the object of his words couldn't make them out in any case.

"Right, dear colleague," he said then, still holding on to the young man who, blushing up to his ears, was asking himself how far the people in this town would go to humiliate him. "Didn't you see my wife?"

What have I got to do with your wife? Mr. Bardócz thought to himself, and he would have given up an increase in pay for a clever, diplomatic way to insult the titulary headmaster.

"Isn't she at home?" he asked, having nothing more intelligent to say.

"No, she isn't."

"That's odd! ..."

He realized he'd said something strange by the way Mr. Veres's small, black, restless eyes, which had scanned the entire length and breadth of the street, now fixed themselves again on him.

Veres expected no further response, as he'd seen the moment Bardócz had opened his mouth that he knew nothing of his wife; in a fit of embarrassment, he slowly released the button on the young man's coat.

After so many indignities, the young colleague began to feel good about himself. "He's a sly old fox," he praised himself in the third person over the bitter pill he'd so cleverly administered. Even the most innocent woman could acquire a reputation from a single casual remark! ... And after all who knew, perhaps there were no innocent women upon the earth.

Veres, God knows why, didn't dare pursue the matter any further, but instead quickly reached for his colleague's hand, barely touching it, and rushed off.

"Dammit, I've got to hurry. Where can I find my wife? The poor curate is waiting at my place ... What does this man mean? ... Why 'odd'? ... Surely she's at the Dvihallys'. I'll go there ... Why would that be odd? ... A wife can leave the house after all! ... Odd!"

He continued distractedly on his way and didn't realize until the last moment that, on the opposite side, the mayor was headed towards him. In his fear that he might neglect to express the proper greeting, he lifted his hat so high as to be entirely out of proportion with the tense relationship between them. There was a good deal of bad blood between the two of them in matters pertaining to the school, and he didn't want the mayor to think he was afraid of him. And yet there went the pudgy, pot-bellied little mayor along as though he were already the victor. This prompted Veres to decide for once and for all to write the biting article for the *World* newspaper that would expose the entire clique that was causing so much trouble around the place ...

From the tobacconist's window, the owner's daughter, Rozika, was leaning on her elbows and peering out into the street. She was a lovely young girl, though full of freckles. Suddenly it seemed to him that he must greet the girl.

"Hello, Rozika," he greeted the former pupil, who in her haughtiness thought it inappropriate to greet the older man first. "Do you all have this sort of thing?"

"What is it?" the girl asked, her curiosity aroused.

"This, have a look!" And not a moment later he'd clicked open the automatic lighter in front of her snubby little nose.

Rozika released an affected cry and withdrew her head in exaggerated fear. "My, how you frightened me!"

"What's the matter?" the tobacconist's wife asked, rushing over to them.

"It's an automatic lighter! Something you don't have in your store, my good lady!" And the educator cheerfully clicked the lighter open and shut.

"Why of course we stock such things, why wouldn't we? At two crowns and fifty fillers a piece."

"Impossible!"

"Bring them here, Rozi. These exact ones!"

Rozika retrieved two such lighters and brought them. The teacher eyed them in amazement.

"Indeed," he said. "They're one and the same! One and the same!"

"Two crowns fifty fillers."

"Unheard of. Everyone's swindling me!"

"How much did you pay for yours, then, Mr. Veres?" Rozika boldly asked.

"I'm ashamed to say it. Truly ashamed, by God. Five crowns."

"My God! That can't be!" the tobacconist's wife proclaimed, clapping her hands together, as did her daughter. "Doubtless from some itinerant salesman!" the lady added.

"Dammit. Well, it doesn't matter! ... Have you by chance seen my wife?"

"No," the lady responded hesitantly. "Right, Rozi, we haven't seen her?"

"I would have had to see her, as I've been here all morning long."

"I kiss your hand," Veres said in elegant German, and returned the lighter to her. "So they've taken me with this, too. That's all right. More was lost in the Battle of Mohács ... Surely my wife is over at Dvihally's. I'll go there now."

"That could be, but she didn't come this way. Maybe she went by way of the alley."

He held his own lighter in his hand and once again crossed to the other side of the street. There were no customers at the barber's, and beardless Pecsenye came out from behind the mosquito curtain to approach the teacher.

"At your service, teacher sir! Wouldn't you like to come inside?"

The educator stroked his stubbly chin, which he was accustomed to shaving himself each morning, and said:

"No ... But look here, how upsetting, I bought this lighter – " In that moment he noticed that his cigar had gone out. He removed it from his mouth and stuffed it into his coat pocket. "I was swindled with it."

"Surely not!" the barber said, having transformed from a businessman to an empathetic human being.

"I paid five crowns for it, and the local tobacconist sells it for two crowns fifty."

"Outrageous! In fact, it's criminal!" the barber said, horrified. At bottom, though, he felt no real sympathy, because in reality it's not so simple to separate the businessman from the empathetic friend. And the teacher only came in every couple of weeks to get his hair cut, paying only thirty-five to forty kreutzers each time. So he hadn't earned a great deal of sympathy; but some sympathy was in fact called for, as a new barber had set up shop in Gödi Út, the street where the teacher lived, who the barber feared could take from him even this forty kreutzers worth of business.

The teacher departed with a nod of his head and went on his way. A Slovak man from Garam with a wide-brimmed hat approached him. Veres called out to him in Slovak: "Who are you looking for?"

"With respect, *pan urodzeni*,[2] I am looking for *pan doktor*!"

---

[2] noble sir

"What?!" the teacher said and demanded with great interest to know what doctor he was seeking. "The mountebank?"

"Of course, of course, what other sort of doctor could a Hronyec man be looking for?"

The teacher was somewhat annoyed that this Jewish doctor had such a reputation, but on the other hand it pleased him that the Irshava native was making a name for their town even in Garam. He was interested in everything in the world, and so he questioned the peasant concerning the details of his ailment and made a great show of his ability to speak in Slovak!

Then he proceded on his way and sighed to himself again: "Dammit all! Where could my wife be? That poor curate will be bored to tears. He hasn't a single acquaintance here in town, and I left him all by himself. But why did she go to Dvihally's at this time of day? ... What a lovely conversation they could be having if she were at home ... Damned that woman!"

At the corner he entered the co-op shop. This he had started himself, and his feelings for it were as those for his own child would be.

As he stepped inside the shop filled with odors of vinegar, petroleum, herbs, and other indistinguishable smells, he heard a loud noise.

Pista Máté was there, the Reformed teacher from the neighboring village of Druhonyec, and he was storming about wildly. "It's an absolute disgrace to treat a man like that! Who am I, that someone dares do that to me!"

"What are you going on about?" Veres asked, laying one hand on the fellow's shoulder, while with the other he pulled the extinguished cigar back out of his pocket.

The moment Pista Máté noticed the supervisory head of the board of directors, he turned toward him. "Of all the nerve, treating me that way!"

"What's all this?" Veres asked the assistant calmly, cleverly crunching the cigar between his fingers. "I know nothing about it!"

Pista Máté threw his head back.

"Oh, don't go on so!"

"If you please," the assistant interjected, who had been a tanner's apprentice but, since he didn't like the craft and was determined to be a gentleman, had been placed by relatives in the co-op shop as its manager – "if you please, the teacher is upset because we're not willing to hand out goods to the entire village on his own purchase account ledger."

"No, my friend, that surely doesn't work!"

"No? Then I'll quit the co-op shop with the entire village and found the co-op shop of Druhonyec! Then you'll see what nice advantages will slip away from you."

"Oh, please. Come on, let's drink a glass of beer instead."

Pista Máté shrugged his shoulder, on which a hunting rifle hung, pushed his cap back on his head, and led the way. He twirled his small blond mustache between his fingers and left the co-op with a stubborn expression.

As they stepped outside, the tanner's apprentice, now manager, winked to himself.

"He certainly likes his pennies! He wants to get a percentage of the entire village's purchases at year's end ... Why certainly ..."

"Our teacher here doubtless has more purchases to his name than two parsons!" said a woman from Druhonyec in Slovak, to whom the manager sold everything she asked for on the teacher's purchase ledger without the slightest fuss.

The two teachers went inside the gate of the neighboring central tavern.

It was a dry, hot summer, but there never failed to be mud in the courtyard. Dirt and garbage were plentiful below the arched gate. The stench of dung wafted across the courtyard, while the odor of schnaps escaped the tavern's open door on the right.

They entered the broad open corridor through a glass door on the left and went here through the first door into the gentlemen's room.

The domed room was still empty and completely dark.

"Bertácska, Bertácska!" Pista Máté called out, then looked around the room.

A single gentleman was seated at the table. It was the new deputy judge who'd been transferred recently to the local district court. He didn't make an especially friendly impression, as he lacked the rowdy allures by which the good boozing companions quickly recognized one another. On the other hand, it was a good sign that he spent so much time sitting in the tavern. So he wasn't one of those unbearable bookworms who is capable of sitting alone in a room for years on end.

"Good day, sir!" Pista Máté, who knew exactly how to tip his hat with everyone he encountered, greeted the man.

"Good evening!" the deputy judge replied, indicating with a nod that they should have a seat.

"Lovely summer we're having!" Máté said, and set his rifle by his feet.

"What kinds of things do you hunt now, teacher sir?" the deputy judge asked.

"Now? Now I hunt men!" Máté answered, tossing back his splendid, swaggering head with serious, burning eyes.

"Confound it! Let's have a light."

Veres listened in silence, as he felt terrible; again he recalled his wife and the curate, who was waiting for him at home ... He took out his automatic lighter.

"Here, have a light ..."

"What sort of a gadget have you got there?" Máté asked.

"I was swindled. I paid five crowns for it."

"Five?" the deputy judge asked, lighting up – "then I'm the one who got swindled. I paid seven for one."

"Hahaha!" Veres laughed with a roar. "That's good, then! Then I wasn't swindled after all!" And he, too, lit up his Puerto Rican cigar.

Máté took the lighter and inspected it. "A strange bit of foolishness!"

"You can buy one from the tobacconist for one forint twenty kreutzers a piece."

"Expensive!" Máté exclaimed.

"Expensive? When I paid five crowns for it?"

"And I seven?"

"Certainly, my friend, when one is a gentleman, then one spends five crowns for it, even seven! But for me to go to the tobacconist's and buy one? And pay one forint twenty – that's expensive! Think how many matches I can get for one forint twenty kreutzers."

Everyone laughed, agreeing with him.

Bertácska came. A young lady. She was a blonde, plump, fragrant girl, no longer terribly young, no longer terribly innocent, but everyone knew she had twenty thousand crowns in the bank. The tavern keeper was infatuated with her and from ten in the evening on he sprang for beer, wine, and occasionally champagne on his own account. This aroused such esteem for her that the gentlemen always gave her twice the usual tip. And they never asked anything of her.

"A glass of beer, Bertácska!"

"One for me too."

Bertácska turned on the electric lamp and carried herself with the imperturbability of a housewife.

"It's not worthwhile for the gentlemen to sit in the dark if no women are present."

"Sit here with us, Bertácska!" Mr. Veres said with a tickle, and he clicked his tongue, gave a little wink, and gave the deputy judge a knowing look.

"I'll sit with you, but first I'll bring the beers!" She sauntered off.

"You old rogue!" Máté remarked, slapping Veres on the shoulder.

Veres smiled as though he'd received a great compliment.

"When you've got such a beautiful wife!" Máté said, wrapping his arm around his friend's neck and giving him a shake. "You sly dog! Needs some cashierwomen to ogle! What does your wife have to say about that? A fabulous wife! And young!"

"Did you perhaps get married recently?" the judge asked.

"You don't know his wife, judge sir? Ah, a splendid woman. I don't understand how this old dog got hold of her."

Veres just kept smiling. This silent, satisfied smile suited him, it gave his face a certain paternal intimacy.

"Do you gentlemen know the new curate?" he asked, suddenly animated.

"He's already here?"

"Yes. He's at my place. I left him there. I brought him so I could introduce him to my wife, but of course my wife wasn't at home, so I told the curate to wait there a few minutes, I would go and find my wife ..."

"You're certainly looking in the right place here!" Máté laughed.

"A splendid young man!"

"The curate?"

"My wife will like him!"

"Why?"

"I just think she will. Why wouldn't she? He's a good man. Quiet. And clever too. A learned, remarkable young man. We did well to get him. And handsome too."

"Goodness me! Won't he be too much?"

"Hardly, as I'll be catching it as it is from my wife ... Dammit, if they would just bring that beer."

The deputy judge eyed the two teachers thoughtfully. He was thinking of Madame Bovary, of this case that was so amazing, but would never occur again. A woman of that magnitude could not be found in this town ... For someone to undergo such a drastic development required a grand cultural environment ... What a caricature is this world in which we live, a caricature of a caricature ... the epitome of ordinariness. Dull, monotonous ordinariness. Where are those colors, those moods whose traces still filled the hazy memory of the small French town he'd encountered in the pages of the book ... There life had color and fragrance ... But here everything is so sober and plain ... nothing could be more ordinary than an act of infidelity in this society ...

He pursed his lips acridly and looked from his corner at the two alienating men. He could imagine this ordinary, neat young teacher entering a relationship with the older man's wife, but this thought itself destroyed his illusions: it struck him that the life that surrounded him made life itself impossible.

"Well, I can't wait for Bertácska," Veres said suddenly.

"It appears a fresh keg is being tapped!" Máté remarked.

"So stay and drink, my friends. I have to go. In any case it's not acceptable for me to leave the young man alone like that ... I've got to get my wife. But look, judge sir, come and visit us some time. We'd love to see you. It would make my wife very happy."

"Yes, well, if ..." the judge replied hesitantly, not knowing what to do or how to decline the invitation.

"No 'if.' The day after tomorrow we'll expect you for dinner. Yes? We're having a dinner for the young curate, that is, we're inviting a few good acquaintances. All very good people ... You'll come as well?"

"My friend, I can't leave Druhonyec every day ..."

"Of course! ... In that case, farewell." He took his hat from the hook, grabbed his walking stick, then offered his hand with great dignity to the deputy judge and with convivial friendliness to Máté. Then he bowed once more and left.

"Teacher sir, teacher sir! Where are you going? You wouldn't leave your fresh beer behind!" Bertácska came, bringing three glasses of frothy beer.

"Confound it!" Veres cried jokingly. "Hand it over."

"It's very good."

"I wouldn't care if it were poison! Just let me have it!" and he drained his glass in one go and with a twinkle in his eye gave it back to the girl, who waited for it with a smile.

"Right? It was good? And to think you were going to leave it behind!"

"Nothing doing! ... Here's your money."

"Your wife just passed by the tavern, teacher sir!"

"What the deuce! Then I really must go! Gentlemen, I wish you good day!" With comical haste he slipped out the door. As he disappeared into the darkness outside, he looked even smaller than he truly was.

"The old fool!" Máté chuckled, shaking his head. "But his wife – what an intriguing woman!"

"Who is it then? I don't know her!" the deputy judge said.

"How could you not know her?" Bertácska blurted out. "She's always wearing this broad, flat, red hat."

"A blonde!" the judge said thoughtfully.

"Not a blonde, a brunette!" Máté said.

"What are you talking about? So her hair may be brown, but she gives the impression of a blonde ... She has very white skin. And a gold tooth."

"Aha. A gold tooth. And large, lively, mocking eyes!"

"Yes, exactly! That's her!"

"A splendid woman!" Máté repeated, then downed half his beer.

"I know a good story about her," Bertácska began. "A short time ago she was visiting her parents, and when she arrived there, the maid received her with the news that the piglets had croaked! To that she said – she clapped her hands together and said: 'Thank God!'"

Máté knew this story well, nevertheless he burst out laughing anew.

"A splendid lady!" the cashierwoman said. "She didn't like to feed the piglets and her husband forced her to ... 'Thank God they croaked!' That's what she said."

The deputy judge was stunned. The few words had an extraordinary effect on him. As though a magic wand had momentarily parted, like a dirty sea, the smutty waves of ordinary life, allowing him to glimpse in a flash of lightning the countless intriguing treasures lurking in life's depths ...

"How did they get together?" he asked.

"Via the mail. She was a poor, noble girl and worked at the post office. She was the postmaster's employee. But she didn't like working there. It wasn't just feeding the piglets that she didn't like! ..."

Bertácska's face soon expressed the disparagement with which the bourgeois women look down on the person who says "Thank God!" over the death of a piglet ... And the judge suddenly saw life through this little crack with such rosey colors that his lust for living and an illusion-inducing mood overcame him! And abruptly he decided he must go to the dinner without fail. He wanted to see her up close, wanted to get a good look at this woman, compared with whom the restaurant cashier was a primitive philistine who'd gone sour.

In the mean time, Veres had caught up with his wife. "My child!" he called after her.

"Well?" she responded, coming to a stop.

"I've been looking for you as though I were searching throughout the entire town for a needle. Where have you been?"

"Where? Why I've been at the Dvihallys'! Where else should I be?"

Veres would gladly have stood arm in arm with her, but she stood so coolly before him that he didn't dare push her to snub him in a public street.

"I brought the young curate home to introduce to you."

"I'm glad," the lady said, pursing her lips.

"He's waiting there at our home, because I went after you ..."

"I don't understand why you would leave someone at our home like that! Everything's in such disorder. How could you leave him there? Couldn't you have waited until I got home?"

The man felt that his wife was once again completely right, and he didn't dare open his mouth. His thoughts wandered back and forth, then suddenly a single question commanded his attention: What had Bardócz meant with the word "odd"? Then he said out loud: "The new deputy judge has promised to come and have dinner with us the day after tomorrow."

"Really?" his wife asked, surprised.

She didn't say another word on the way home. The husband would have liked to find out what was on her mind. But that was out of the question. A man can't figure out what's occupying his wife's thoughts.

But when they turned onto Gödi Street, he had an idea. "My child, I left the curate in the library. He's been sitting there reading. He wouldn't go into the other rooms."

He looked searchingly at his wife's face, which he could see very well, since they were standing below the electric street light, but he saw nothing there.

Again he would have liked to link his arm in his wife's, but this simple gesture was out of the question.

He merely wrinkled his brow beneath his stiff hat and shuffled alongside the woman with a long face.

II

After dinner, Mr. Veres said: "Nothing's better than being at home. A man feels good at home, not worrying about anything; my wife is here, my good friend, my nephew, everything around me is dear to me, even the furniture I know so well. That bookcase belonged to my grandfather, the poor man was a minister until the day he died. The chair where you're sitting, my young curate friend, that chair is at least a hundred years old. But it's still so sturdy, that if I had the cabinetmaker Makovics make one today it would be a piece of junk in comparison."

He paused as he was having trouble with his cigar. He began drawing on it forcefully, took it from his mouth, put it back in, then took a paper cigar holder out of his pocket, carefully pressed the cigar into it, and reinserted it between his tobacco-stained teeth.

"I mean, everything's so much more expensive these days," the curate put in.

"No, no, I tell you no." Veres picked up his glass and raised it to propose a toast. The curate lifted his as well, as did the teacher's nephew, the student who took room and board with him and was likewise no slacker – he too held up his glass, but in the last moment the curate paused and turned toward the lady of the house:

"Please, dear lady, join us in our toast."

The young woman sat in her spot and listened to the conversation while leaning on her elbows. She released a laugh, and her right eye tooth, which was of gold, twinkled brightly. "You'll soon have me drunk," she said.

Her husband burst out laughing. "A woman is truly beautiful when she lets her hair down!" he cried. "Drink up, dear, for cripes sake!"

The curate held the glass obligingly toward her, his young, round face already blushing from the wine. His eyes sparkled and his thin, blond moustache curled itself all the way around to the base of his nose. He looked at the lady just then as though she were his older sister, or perhaps his ideal or the favored object of his adoration. The woman felt the rays of his manly ardor gleaming toward her.

She took the glass and, with a blend of motherly superiority and feminine coquetry, clinked it with his!

"You don't know how to clink glasses. You don't know how to clink glasses!" the curate said, meaning that one must look into the other's eyes when the glasses touch!

The lady's smile grew, and as she lifted her glass to her mouth, she looked into the curate's eyes as though to say: "Even such children actually do know a thing or two!" Then she continued to sit, leaning now not just on one but on both her elbows. The curate emptied his glass and looked at the woman with a radiant expression, as though wanting to impress her with his heroic drinking abilities.

And he saw how the lady's bossom swelled between her two arms, and the thought overcame him – more intoxicating than any wine – of how it would be to stand and reach around the lady from behind, beneath her armpits, and grasp the orbs of her chest with his palms!

The master of the house drank like a turkey, with eyes closed. After he drank, he blinked once or twice, then went on imparting his wisdom.

"If I may, that's not how it is. Whether something is more expensive now than it was a hundred years ago is very difficult to say. When my grandfather had furniture made for his daughter, he chopped down two old walnut trees in the garden, and brought in a cabinet maker with family in tow, who worked for him into the spring. And there he lived with his five children. I humbly admit, I have no idea how much money he paid him ..."

"It can't have been much!" the curate put in. He said it with a laugh, just so he could contradict him for once, but the teacher took it as a provocation. His face grew stern and with a smack of his lips he drew his moustache all the way down to his chin.

"No, it can't have been much," he agreed, "that's a fact, but I humbly ask that you consider what it requires to provide for a family throughout the winter: a cabinet maker with his wife, plus the five children, nowadays! Hardly child's play!"

He looked the curate in the eye seriously, decisively; only his eyelids twitched, a sign of the wine's beginning to speak for him.

"Hardly!" agreed the curate, for although he was fond of teasing, of bandying words like a schoolboy, he thought twice about doing so his first time here, in a strange new place, and above all in the presence of a beautiful lady! ... After all, he was in reality not a serious, self-reliant man, but a mere student ... And what a beautiful lady! Again he looked at her and observed her dark eyes, her rosy, beige skin, the blood visible beneath it, her mocking red mouth – only the gold tooth disturbed him! And her ample breasts! which again caused his eyes to glaze over.

He looked back at the teacher and repeated once more: "That was hardly child's play!" Then he began to wonder what had occasioned his saying that. He'll drink himself tipsy yet! And that would be a disaster! To get stewed his first time in the presence of such a splendid lady. He must leave tomorrow, flee from here! ... Or, better yet, this very evening ...

The teacher was touched that the curate had twice now agreed with him. He lifted his glass, but noticed then that it was empty.

"Hey fellow," he cried out to his nephew, "are you asleep?"

The student sat quietly at the end of the table, hoping no one would notice he was still there and hadn't long since left to attend to his work, his studies. He got up, went over to the sideboard, took the wine bottle from the tray and, one after the other, proceded to fill each person's glass.

"Look how the fellow lounges about! By George! His examinations are about to begin, and instead of holing himself up like a diligent student should and drilling his *hic, haec, hoc*, he lounges about over here. What will become of those *matura* exams of yours?"

The student shot a terrible look of disdain at his uncle, who was merely a primary school teacher and therefore had no idea what *hic, haec, hoc* was. He smiled and, with the self-respect of the learned man, said:

"We'll get through it one way or another!"

"I know that a squash turns yellow in the sun, but that still won't make a melon out of it!" his uncle teased him, and everyone was impressed by what an excellent shot he'd taken at his nephew. They even laughed at the snub, to the point where the uncle thought the shame too great, and he took out his watch.

"Ten o'clock," he said. "My my, how the time has flown. And we didn't even notice it."

"Although you certainly could have noticed it based on the amount of wine inside you by now," the lady said.

"It's not even that much!" the man returned seriously, sensing keenly that his wife was speaking with him, here in

39

front of other people, in the same way that he was speaking with his nephew.

"No, it isn't much!" the curate said with flashing eyes, his gaze fixed fast upon the lady.

Again it pleased the teacher that the curate expressed such agreement, and he exclaimed: "Well, then let's have another drink! You too, young man, may empty yet another glass of wine with us, but after that I ask that you please withdraw and give science its due ..."

And they drank. The teacher took just a sip so that his wife wouldn't get upset with him. The curate took two sips, while the student drained his glass completely. No matter, it was all he was going to get!

"You should drink as much of the wine of science, dear nephew, as you do of my wine!" the teacher said, finishing the thought he'd begun, then laughed out loud.

The student turned red, upon which he said good night and quickly left.

"How wonderful these student years are," the teacher remarked once his nephew had left the room, "the most wonderful years of one's life. Nonetheless I wouldn't want to be a student again."

All three of them laughed.

"When I think that tomorrow I'd have to go to class and recite in pedagogy, God knows I'd fail."

"It's a wonderful thing indeed when a man can say that he has no more exams to sit!" the curate stated with heartfelt conviction.

"So you still have examinations to sit?" the lady asked.

"Yes, milady, unfortunately I do. The theological examination is behind me. Now I'm pressing ahead with the professional exam."

"When will that take place?"

"A year from now."

"Well, then be sure to study hard between now and then."

"Hahaha!" the teacher roared with laughter. "A curate and studying! What a farce! A curate must study something entirely different. To pay court – that's what he's got to learn … There are girls enough around here!"

The curate looked over at the lady's bossom and once again his eyes glazed over.

For the second time the lady noticed this look, and now she figured out what it meant. Immediately she made an unconscious movement, leaning back in her chair and stretching out her arms. The curate followed her motions with misty eyes and drank in the new roundnesses of the woman's breasts with such dread and shame that the lady blushed and cast a glance at her husband, to see if he noticed anything.

But for all his cleverness the husband noticed nothing and continued talking incessantly.

"A curate is already a full-fledged man. He's no longer a student. He has other work to do. My dear friend, in life we have need of entirely different things from what are taught in school. One could say," he bellowed, carried away by his own train of thought, "that in life we need only that of which no knowledge is taught in school! The most important thing being love! What does a person learn about that in school? And then there's making money! The devil would take anyone who wanted to teach how to make money in school. And then there's earning respect! That, too, requires something besides learning one's school lessons!"

"Splendid!" the lady pronounced. "They teach those other subjects in school, because everyone knows these things for themselves. It's those other things that have to be learned!"

For a moment it was as though the question had been clarified for them, which would have made all three of them happy. But then the teacher started analyzing the notion.

"What? Latin? And Greek? Is that something we need to know?"

The curate likewise regarded the wife, asking her with his eyes whether they needed to know those things.

The lady merely sneered. "Of course we do! Whoever can't manage to learn those is nothing but a big ass and will certainly never become a parson. Nor even a gentleman, he'll simply remain a craftsman. That's why young people have to study diligently, so they can join the upper class, where one can live well. If a man doesn't learn Latin and Greek, how could he dare court a gentlewoman!"

"And that's the main thing!" the teacher cried with a loud laugh.

In this moment, the curate pardoned the school for all its Latin classics, and he pardoned religion for the Bible that was written in Greek and Hebrew.

The man of the house reached for his glass and offered a toast.

"Your servant!" he proclaimed to the curate.

The young man turned red up to his ears, he was deeply touched that the teacher, who was at least twice his age, thus invited him to use the familiar "*te*" form of address with him. It was his first time to be on first name terms with a real man. A married man! One who had such a gorgeous wife into the bargain.

"I feel so honored, teacher sir!" he stammered with great emotion, then in the next moment he was ashamed for getting so emotional. What! After all, he was already a curate. And one day he'd regret being on such familiar terms with a primary school teacher. Well, it's not so bad in the end, he quickly comforted himself! He's got a beautiful wife! ...

He clinked glasses with the husband and immediately looked over towards the wife, who witnessed his discomfort with a smile. The gentle, pious little man who could blush like a girl pleased her more and more. She reached her glass toward him coquettishly.

"So you see," she said, "it's good that you learned Greek, right?"

The curate felt like he was in a steam bath. A sensuous torpor flooded his body and he grew faint. He saw the lady only as through a veil, and it was clear to him that he was falling mortally in love with this splendidly beautiful woman. His lips opened and were inflamed with red as he uttered in a hoarse voice: "Yes, milady."

III

The student entered his room where the lamp had burned vainly in his absence, and within a moment it was clear to him that he had no desire to do any work today. Horace lay open on his desk, he began to read the next ode:

> *O navis referent in mare te novi*
> *fluctus, o quid agis? fortiter occupa*
> *portum! nonne vides ...*

Then he perused the study guide, scanning the text with impatient haste ... : "Oh ship, new waves shall bring you back to the shore. Oh, what are you doing? Conquer the harbor with force. Don't you see that your sides are divested of the ruddering crew and your mast is yet wounded by swift Africus and your sailyards creak, and without their ropes, hulls can barely withstand the mightier sea? None of your sails is intact, you have no gods whom you, repeatedly beset by misfortune, can call on for help. No matter that you are the offspring of Pontine firs from a noble wood, you appeal in vain to your origins, your name: the fearful sailor has no faith in the painted bow. Beware of becoming the plaything of the waves. You, who were recently the object of my worried ruminations, and are now the object of my desire and of my not inconsequential concern, I beg you to circle around the sprawling waters of the Cyclades."

He turned the page only to see that the ode ended there. He regarded the Latin text and sought out a word from which he could establish that it really ended like that; the last word *Cycladas*: in the study guide "Cyclades" ... the end.

He sighed in relief, because as he was reading it, this ode weighed down on his brain like a leaden helmet, compressing his medullary substance and immersing the entire world before him in fog. Suddenly he thought of a boat in which they'd paddled among the reeds down the Sajó River last summer, and a wave of clarity rushed across his head like a gale clearing away the fog. He saw vividly the big brown boat with its iron mountings tinged red by rust. Then he imagined an ocean vessel sailing for America. With great longing he thought how splendid it would be to go to America and live there. He would learn English and have that same ample clothing made for him as the American Hungarian who was recently in school looking for his brother.

All this lasted only a moment. While he thought of these things, his eyes were as though clouded over and the letters grew hazy before him. In the meantime, his vision again cleared and the Latin poem stood sharply profiled on the page. With revulsion he studied it and thought how many instances of the *genitivus partitivus* and the *gerundium absolutum* must be found in this poem. Dizziness overcame him anew and he was forced to look away. He scanned to himself:

O-na viss-refe rent! In mare te novi ...

Once they had learned this ode by heart, but now he could remember only the first few lines. He also knew that the first two lines were called "Asclepiadic" verses.

He heaved a deep sigh.

"That curate has got it good, though," he thought to himself, "drinking in there and fixing his gaze on my aunt."

Anger took hold of him. He was consumed with hatred of this small-moustached youth, who had the right to look at his aunt in a way that was off limits to him. He grew jealous and imagined that his own right to love his aunt was both older and greater than that of anyone in the world. Her husband had no right to her. He was a shriveled and utterly uncultivated man who was incapable of understanding this woman. Nor did any of the others have a right. Neither Dvihally, nor Pál Csorba, nor the parson, nor any of the others who were constantly fluttering about his aunt. It struck him at least that every man who so much as laid eyes on this lady immediately fell in love with her.

He still had no desire to sit and work. He got up from the table and strode across the room. He stood at the window and looked out. Then he opened it ...

His forehead was red, burning, the wine threatened to burst through it, and somewhere in the depths of his nerves he sensed a powerful tension.

"Awful. As if I were in a prison."

He stretched again and tried to comfort himself with the knowledge that, within a month, he would be a free man. By then his *matura* exam would be behind him and the tortures of school would cease to agonize him at least for the time being.

"I wonder if Gacsal has already bought the latest issue of *Fidibusz*[3]?" he asked himself. He was overcome by terrible sexual arousal and immediately decided to pay Gacsal a visit.

He donned his hat and quickly slipped outside. Once he'd closed the door behind him, he gloated in the feeling that he'd again left old Horace locked up in his room.

He hurried down the stairs on tiptoe.

In the courtyard the ground crunched and crackled beneath his feet, he was afraid the noise would be heard from above, but singing sounded through the window from the upper floor. All three of them were singing there in the room. For a moment he stood and listened to the woman's

---

[3] A satirical weekly published in Budapest.

voice, as his aunt's was clearly distinguishable from the others. They were singing the new song:

> I would love to see your face once more,
> Once more to wait for hours in the street,
> Once more to kiss the happiness I've lost!
> Afterwards my lust will die away ...

The blood rushed to his head and he nearly fainted. The curate's voice trotted along behind his aunt's. Clearly he was now learning this song. Terrible rage took hold of him. He himself had taught the song to his aunt, and now the unfaithful beast was teaching it to this detestible curate! He felt that one day he would box that curate's ears so hard that blood would pour from his nose and mouth!

After the song there was laughter. Surely they were praising the song for its beauty.

And he had to hear all that from a distance ... He lowered his hat over his forehead, then left with hurried steps.

He went out onto the street. Once he reached the corner from where he could still see the window, he turned and stared at it. The little window shone yellow from the old building, which looked as gloomy as a fortress in the night. But holding sway in the small, brightly-lit space behind it was a merriment that caused him the most hellish of torments. Doubtless the curate is ogling his aunt now with even greater abandon, perhaps he's even touching her hand! Or, beneath the table, her foot! or her leg. Since this slippery rogue is capable of anything.

And from this small foundation his fantasy made the most fearsome leap. He pictured anything and everything the curate could possibly do with his aunt.

Sweat pearled on his forehead, and he was terribly relieved to know that, if he himself was not there, at least his uncle was in the room with them! Thanks to this, there was no reason to fear for the lady, it was so good to know that that impassive man guarded his wife like a eunuch ...

Someone placed a hand on his shoulder.

He turned around. It was *Hounddog*, his professor.

In an instant, he metamorphosed into a submissive student.

"So, my friend," the teacher said, placing his pince-nez beneath his eyebrows and peering through them with half-open mouth. "Well, where are we off to? Where are we off to?"

"If you please, professor sir, my Horace vocabulary list is with Gacsal, so I'm going to his place to get it."

"I see, so you're translating Horace now?"

"Yes."

"The odes?"

"Yes."

"Very smart. And which one are you doing now?"

The student was seized by the vain hope that the professor would not forget this encounter at the time of the examination, thus with even greater student subservience, he said:

"The fourteenth, professor sir. 'O navisrefe-rent!' ..."

"Yes, that's right. And the vocabulary list is with Gacsal."

"Yes, because he's been translating Horace as well."

"He's been translating him? When?"

"I think he's already finished today."

"Yes. One must work through all the material for the entire four years. My son, the *matura* is an important matter. The commissioner is coming, a very stern man, and one can never know what he will ask. So no lolling about. This one time you've got to summon all your strength. Maintain both discipline and focus!"

"Thank you kindly ..." the student said in a tone filled to the brim with childlike innocence. Whoever could pronounce these three words like that could not possibly have anything on his mind besides the rules of Latin syntax.

"Just go quickly to get your vocabulary list and then immediately back home. Study! Study! Study! Let me remind you that with a single false step you put everything at risk – your entire future is at stake."

With a nod of his long, black-hatted head, the professor left. The student drew his head between his shoulders and, his soul filled with awe, rushed to Gacsal's place.

The gate was already closed, so he knocked.

Soon he heard footsteps, then someone opened the gate. It was the maid. In the moment when he stepped inside, he brushed against the girl. It was as though an electric current coursed through him – all his blood rushed to his head.

The girl closed the gate. The student stood there and waited with bloodshot eyes. His throat was parched.

"Pardon me, is the young man at home?"

"The young man? No, he's not."

"He's not?" the student repeated, utterly distraught. "Where is he?"

"At his grandparents' home."

"At his grandparents' home?" His voice was so dry that the sounds seemed to scrape past each other.

They merely stood there for a moment.

"Would you like to come inside the house?" asked the girl.

"No!" the student replied, but with such indecision that he himself didn't know if he meant yes or no.

"No?"

Again they just stood there.

"I won't come in!" the student said again forcefully.

"As you wish."

"Who is at home?"

"No one, just me."

"No one?"

"They all went to the grandparents' home, as they're celebrating name day there."

It occurred to the student that today was the day for celebrating the name Robert. Gacsal's grandfather was named Robert, Robert Gacsal. Hesitantly, he approached the gate.

The girl followed him quietly.

"Wouldn't you like to wait for him? The young man will be home right away, as he has to study."

"No," the student said in alarm. "I've got to hurry as well, since I have to study."

He was already at the gate. He felt faint. His mouth fell open and remained open as he stood there.

While the girl opened the gate once more, he stared mechanically at her neck, which shone white in the dark. It was as round as that of a Greek statue, but warmer ... hotter.

"Wouldn't you like for me to tell him something?"

"My vocabulary list ..." the student choked forth, but then it occurred to him how things stood with this vocabulary list. "No, nothing!"

With this he quickly left through the gate.

"G'night, then!" the girl called after him, but he didn't reply.

Panting and out of breath, he stormed ahead.

At the corner, he stopped. He shivered, his knees and hands shook. He ran his hand across his forehead which was dripping with sweat, then he struck himself forcefully in the face.

"What a coward I am! What an ass!"

He bit his lip bloody and gnashed his teeth. "I could have had this girl, and here I am just leaving her there."

He felt ashamed, and sad as well, but what he regretted most was the loss of this prey.

He dug his hands into his pockets and slunk along with lowered head.

He began to analyze what had happened and realized that the girl had been very happy when he'd come and had quickly closed the gate behind him, then was sad when he'd left and had opened the gate for him only slowly. All of this meant that she would gladly have spent the evening alone with him. She'd tried to hold him back. Horror of horrors: and he had let the prey slip through his hands. Tears welled in his eyes and ran hot down his face.

"What's the matter?" someone asked him.

"My aunt is ill," he answered before seeing clearly who it was.

"Really? ..." the headmaster asked him with a sympathetic tone.

The headmaster of the grammar school was a tall, thin man with austere features who expressed sympathy with everyone. He recorded bad grades with the greatest sympathy of all. The students all called him "Lamb's Tail."

The student now recognized his voice. He looked up and glanced fearfully at the headmaster's white-hued face, at his black moustache which curved just as symmetrically as an ox's horns. His Adam's apple rose and fell heftily beneath his high collar.

"And you're coming from her now?" the headmaster asked.

"No, if you please, I'm going to her."

"Well, young man," the headmaster smiled, "there's no need to become desperate as yet. I saw the old woman a few days ago, and she was perfectly well. What's wrong with her?"

"Emphysema."

"Ah, not really such a dangerous illness. She can live with that for a long time yet. And I advise you not to neglect your studies over that — your aunt, the poor dear, can live for many years, but as for you, if you fail your examinations, then I don't know what you'll do."

He laughed as he made this last remark, as though he were saying something humorous.

"Yes, sir," the student said, shuddering.

"So go ahead and see your aunt, and greet her for me as well, wish her good health for me, but then go quickly home. It's time to study, my young friend. It really isn't nice of your aunt to cause her nephew such anxiety during the night. Now we are very strict, as the smallest misstep can bear the most serious of consequences."

He said this like a threatening rebuke. The student turned red.

"But if you please, if my aunt ..."

"All right! I won't say a word, but do rush back home. It's late, respectable students don't wander about in the streets at this time of night."

He nodded and went on his way.

The student shuddered in heated agitation. He knew that these two men, Hounddog and the headmaster, spent every night searching through all the taverns and wandering ceaselessly through the streets in order to catch the students drinking.

"How frightful it is in this beastly little town," he said, "where every person knows the other!"

With this he rushed in the direction of his aunt's home.

Suddenly there appeared before him on the opposite side of the street the building where Víg's room was found. This was the most ill-reputed grammar-school student haunt in the entire city. He'd only been there once, during the daytime, but now an irresistible urge overcame him to go inside.

The gate was open.

The students' room was located in the back of the courtyard. Four young men lived there.

As he entered the room from the courtyard, a cloud of smoke hit him in the face. The place was full of people, at first he was unable to recognize who they all were. Four beds of pine stood in the room, alongside a table, several chairs, a chest of drawers and four trunks, the extent of the furnishings. The youths were lounging around, two to three on a bed. None of those seated in the chairs was sitting properly, instead they were rocking back and forth sprawled across them, all of them smoking cigarettes, and on the chair next to the stove stood a bottle half-filled with wine. It stood there so that, in case of need, it could swiftly be made to disappear.

"Who's that? Who's that?" several called out. "Look, it's Veres! What's he doing here?"

None of them came up to greet him, in fact some of them just turned their backs toward him, while another laughed directly in his face.

"It's the spy!" somebody yelled out.

The blood rose to Laci Veres's face.

"Who's the scoundrel!" he cried. "It's you who's the spy!"

The boys laughed.

"Good then," said one of them.

"Come, have a seat," said Kovács, one of the roommates, and he made space for him on the bed.

Laci sat down in the middle, between two students.

"Have you got a cigarette?" Kovács asked.

"Yes." He got his cigarette case out and handed it to him. Kovács took one. The gangly Smidek, who lay stretched across this same bed and was also a head of the household, reached with his big paw into the case and took out three cigarettes!

"Look at that chiseler!" Palotay cried, and although he was only a guest, he likewise ransacked the cigarette case. He then offered, with due deference, some of his booty to the head man of the lodging, Pista Víg.

As compensation for the pilfered cigarettes, they gave Laci Veres a glass of wine.

One young man intoned a song or other in the far corner of the room. He crooned out the first line solemnly:

> Hey, my bagpiper father
> piped his bagpipes, he did! ...

"Let's really sing something," another guest commanded.

"Let's sing!"

They began with the song: "They mowed the grass in the meadow!" ...

"Is this how you prepare for the *matura* exam?" Laci asked Kovács quietly.

"Ah, my friend, I never encountered a question on that exam that related directly to what I'd studied!" Kovács said with a laugh. He had terribly ugly teeth, each and every one was jagged around the edges.

"Perhaps you're right," Laci replied, and pondered. Then he noticed with surprise that someone was studying at the table in the corner. Szegő was sitting there, a scrawny boy with a lung ailment, working as calmly as though he were alone in the room. They left him in peace, because he wouldn't have let them disturb him in any case. Szegő had, for the past eight years, always lived in the very loudest of rooms, and yet he was the most hard-working, the most pedantic of bookworms, who chewed his way through every subject matter, leaving only the kernel, the intact pieces, the sense of it undigested.

On the other side of the room, they were singing. The elegant Palotay and the strapping Mácsik, who was always laughing and pranking people, soon got together to pow-wow concerning the exam. Everyone had something to say:

"There's no need to get bent out of shape over the *matura*," Reuter put in, "we'll do fine! Once the written part's done, I've only the oral exam to worry about!"

"Don't worry, you'll get the answers whispered to you!" Palotay reassured him.

"Yes, this ruse has met with incredible success!" Mácsik cried.

"Sshhh!"

"What ruse?" Laci Veres asked.

The others roared with laughter.

"You don't know about it yet?"

"We haven't let you and Dávid in on it, because we were afraid you'd turn us in. And you know, you two are the only ones who did the math exam on your own. The others all cheated. Reuter even wrote on his paper: "There was a hole in the disc!" Mácsik laughed with all his might.

Reuter blushed and refuted the accusation.

Across the room the singing grew so loud that it was impossible to understand a single word. Even Kovács caterwauled in his husky voice: "I am like the leaves in fall, tossed about by wind and rain, my life's tree won't last for long, spring will come, and I'll be gone."

The music infected the others as well. Whether with thready or with roaring voice, they all bellowed along.

Laci Veres felt utterly alone and strange. All of these youths had something he lacked: this audacity with which they made their way through life. Each of them knew his position and the role he had to play. They were students living the student life. But he in his quiet seclusion, buried among his little family and a mound of books, felt he didn't belong with them. Not everyone here was a bad student, several of them often gave better answers than he did, but they all had simple souls. It was no secret to any of them what school and its discipline meant; there were assignments that had to be done and others that didn't. They could figure out on what days they would be called on to respond, which they calculated based on all the notes recorded by their names in the professor's notebook. These boys were possessed of a certain roughness, a sense of reality, they weren't confused like he was, their lives weren't tainted with despair as his was ... He sensed that each of these youths would become a man who knew how to duke it out with life. They would become government workers, agriculturalists, merchants, craftsmen, or actors, journalists ... some of them had even indicated these on the school's statistical surveys, which greatly impressed Laci, as he could not commit himself to a single profession and thus indicated simply that he would become a jurist. But why, and what would follow then? ...

Kardos, an ugly, strong Jewish youth whom they'd given the nickname "Hay," stood up and draped a sheet around himself, causing everyone to fall silent. They laughed with curiosity. Kardos wanted to be an actor and would now sing the song of ancient Abraham, performing some silly travesty of everything the students knew concerning the workings of Jewish prayer.

The students were bent over with laughter as Kardos sang:

> Old Abraham has died,
> Hum, hum, hum, hum, hum, hum,
> Hum, hum, hum, hum, hum, hum,
> Old Abraham has died.

He embellished the verse with all the necessary grimaces and antics to make of his performance a true travesty.

> Old Abraham has died …
> And who has buried him? …
> Three Jews that he knew well …
> One of them was Jacob …
> The second one was Isaac …
> The third of them was Moses …
> And where did they put his grave? …
> In the soil of Jerusalem! …

These tomfooleries were unknown to Laci, who was so delighted he could barely laugh.

He was at the end of his years as a student and now must see what a happy world surrounded him, a world of which he knew nothing. His heart stirred with pain, and while the others took in the comedy with bated breath, tears welled in his eyes and his heart hurt.

When the song was over, the students began to yell, "the song of lament, the song of lament!" …

Kardos removed his sheet and, with taut neck, his face distorted by sadness and despair, crooned forth some song about a crying man who does nothing but cry, cry, cry … when he thinks how for a single cutlet an entire ox must be slaughtered! The entire ox … then he cries, he cries and cries …

Then came the third, and then the fourth production. He sawed off the table leg, imitating with remarkable faithfulness the sound of the saw, he improvised an orchestra on the edge of the chest of drawers, and sang the national anthem "To Your Homeland Without Fail Be Faithful, O Hungarian!" in Slovak.

"Will you really become an actor?" Laci asked him when Kardos plopped onto the neighbor's bed after his performance.

"I think I'll become an egg dealer."

"Why?" Laci asked, perplexed.

"I just got a letter from my brother who wrote that I should go to him in Vienna as soon as the exam is over."

"Does he have an egg dealership, then?"

"Yes."

"But what if you still want to become an actor!"

Kardos shrugged his shoulders. "I'd end up only as a low-level comedian." He turned away, poking Kovács in the side, who now stretched himself out across the other end of the bed.

Laci closed his eyes. He didn't understand how someone who wanted to be an actor could also become a merchant ... He stared at Kardos's long nose and wanted to see the reflection of some inner pain there. But the Jewish youth jumped up and butted into Mácsik's story, a sly grin on his face. He told about the cat prank, when they'd gotten a stupid servant to put a dead cat on the teacher's desk. This had happened back when they were in the fifth form; since then the teacher had passed away, but even today every word of the story that called that event to mind inspired uproarious laughter.

All this tumult unfolding before him had Laci utterly beside himself. He ogled Mácsik's plump, handsome white face as though he were looking through a magic lantern. The boy lurched ahead with his story, spluttering as he spoke, getting interrupted at every moment with corrections.

"Aha, aha," he said then, continuing his story with new fire and even greater vehemence: "Remember, my friend, how we took out the stove pipe and filled the classroom with smoke. Then we went into the detention room. We gained at least half an hour. They'd called in every chimney sweep, every handyman, none of whom had been able to help – at least once a day the room was thick with smoke. And one afternoon I was called up to the headmaster, I don't remember why, oh yes, we'd done in all the cats *à la Flaubert*[4] in Vekni Street. So I went into the office, but the headmaster wasn't there. I waited for a bit, then I went out into the hall. That's when I noticed that people were talking in our classroom. Wouldn't you guess, I snuck over

---

[4] Very likely a reference to the satirical animal experiments carried out in Flaubert's unfinished novel *Bouvard et Pécuchet*, first published in 1881 and translated into Hungarian one year later.

there and found the headmaster, along with the caretaker, and a handyman. They were working on the oven. I heard the handyman say repeatedly that there's not a thing wrong with the oven. So why does it smoke so? I just laughed, they should have asked me. – This afternoon it won't smoke, the handyman says. – Good then, the headmaster responds, and I hear him come out. I quickly hide behind the staircase and wait until all three of them have left. Then I slip into the classroom. I pull out the pipe until the entire room is filled with smoke, then I put it back just as pretty as you please and take off. I promptly announce myself to the headmaster. . . . What a nervous wreck he was. Someone should just try to be that cheeky with the headmaster we have now, with Lamb's Tail! ... He grills and grills me, then at last he gets angry: 'Get out,' he says, 'get out, get out of here!' He comes at me, I thought he would hit me, and I retreat to the door, and just when he tries to kick me – he wanted to kick me! – I open the door and his foot slices right through it."

He couldn't go on, he was choking with laughter. The rest, too, were howling so loudly that no one could have understood a single word anyway.

"I left the room then and hid again beneath the staircase. All of a sudden the headmaster comes, with his magnificent limp, I almost burst out laughing ... Then he goes into the room ... He opens the door! My friends, he nearly dropped dead, it was like he had a stroke. There was so much smoke in there ... 'Where's that handyman! Where's that handyman! Get over here, get over here, what's this?' ... But I had to shove off, I just couldn't hold back my laughter anymore."

The boys were all bent over with laughter. When they recovered, the other students joined them. Laci sat in his spot like someone at a bacchanal who refuses to drink and can't understand what's going on around him.

He thought of the two great lies that had slipped out of him today, like wine from a leather bottle when it's pierced.

Albert Reuter took the latest issue of *Fidibusz* from his pocket.

"This is great!" he said, waving the paper about.

Laci's eyes glowed as the lust lurking within him began to surge.

"So much printed rot, what's the point of that," Mácsik said, continuing his role as the focal point in the conversation, "I'll tell you things that no one ever set down on paper!"

And he told some drastic tale that was simply teeming with indecent expressions – everone listened with grinning devotion, the explosive power of their healthy young men's blood all but bursting them apart. But this enormous openness had such a crushing effect on Laci, as though a house were falling in on him. He couldn't bear it. His secretly   nurtured   lustfulness,   his   cellar-grown, underdeveloped lecherousness were burned to the quick by this heat, which was too powerful, too wild and fiery for him. He fared as the pumpkin plant in the sun, he wilted. These never-before-heard, brutish stories caused him not pleasure, but pain and torment. And what hurt him the most was that, in this burning atmosphere, the treasured ideal of womanhood he nurtured within him fell to pieces and vanished before him. It made him want to cry to hear them tell such stories about women, live women, teachers' wives and servants alongside creatures with painted faces known throughout the city, one beside the other indiscriminately ... as though something were breaking to pieces inside him. His body burned, it boiled, and as though it were being transformed into redhot embers, everything that was beautiful and ideal about his image of women burned away in a cloud of sparks ...

"Where am I, then?" he asked himself suddenly and surveyed his companions with nervous eyes.

He saw their red faces, how each one differed from the other. Kovács with his rotten teeth resembled some worm-eaten piece of fruit, while Mácsik's broad, reddened face shone like a poppy blooming in the sun; Kardos drew his long, red nose into a smirk as he tried to commit the anecdotes to memory, and Palotay casually showed his teeth, not the least bit ashamed of how delectably entertained he was by the bawdy tales.

"How depraved they are, dear God, how depraved," Laci said to himself, although he was not so much less depraved as simply unaccustomed to enjoying forbidden fruit without some sense of false shame. Pista Víg, the head student in the room, who'd sat listening the entire evening because he was a dull-witted, commonplace strongman who couldn't string two words together, showed his muscles now, cracking his bones as he stretched. Szegő, yes even Szegő ceased working. Laci noticed how the pen stood still in the consumptive youth's trembling hand, and how red splotches appeared on his face as his eyes stared at the lamp base. To Laci's disgust, the student shuddered in an ecstasy with which even he himself was familiar – the vice that screamed forth from this pathetic youth, for whom everyone knew that such vice had become an illness, horrified him ...

"And yet they all live! They are all living!" Laci's soul cried out to him. "Life belongs to them, because they all know what they seek from life."

And it shamed him to know that he was incapable of being like them. That he would never be a complete man like them. It was as though a celestial wonder sounded in his ear when he heard the young men begin discussing among themselves, with the greatest calm and what impressed him as complete command of the subject matter, whether or not they were full-grown men in the biological sense, whether their seed was fertile as the wheat grains that men sowed in the earth.

He decided it was time to leave this room ...

But for some time he was unable to move.

The conversationalists grew silent for a moment, then Palotay spoke up:

"Word of honor, in Pest there are ladies going about who forcibly drag a man indoors ..."

"Of course," Kardos put in, "what of it?" and he laughed with his immature bass voice.

Again there was silence. Everyone fell deep into thought, then Kovács sighed in a meowing tone: "I'll never get to Pest."

The entire company roared with laughter over this candid remark.

But Laci was already choking with disgust. He was sickened by himself, by life, by men, by women – love as a whole struck him as some execrable ulcer ...

He quickly rose to his feet and offered his fellows his hand.

"Goodbye."

"Goodbye, goodbye," they returned.

"Where are you going?"

"He's going somewhere!" Kardos said.

"I don't recommend it," Palotay put in. "Hounddog has ensconced himself in *that house* now, to the point of even sleeping there. He would die of grief if he didn't catch someone there before the exams. We were there recently, and a girl came up to us and whispered: 'Students, come quickly!' She led us into her room, and we stayed there for half an hour until Hounddog left."

The enormous, feverish, fracturing tension of the midnight hour was terrible. Laci barely managed to stagger outside.

The fresh air restored him somewhat.

When he reached the gate, he was overcome by fear. Surely someone would catch him now. Either the professor, or the headmaster, or the caretaker, as the school attendant had to make his rounds at night in order to lie in wait for wayward students.

He crept forth like a thief. He stopped after every step and peered shivering down the street. The small electric lamps shed scant light, fog began to rise in the air, and by mustering his courage he finally made it as far as Gacsal's home.

"Good night, little maid!" he said softly and blushed.

Ten classmates had met together today in Víg's room, but there wasn't a single one among them who would have passed up the magnificent tidbit that had offered itself voluntarily to his mouth, his lap.

And now it struck him that God himself had led him away from there ... he felt as though he'd kept himself pure of a great sin ... And he did not regret leaving the girl her innocence, he was happy now that he himself remained innocent.

He thought of how one day the maid would marry ... some upstanding man ... how he would unknowingly curse him if ... Then it occurred to him what the boys had said regarding sprouting seeds, and he shuddered. Good God, what danger had threatened him! ... Had he planted a seed and it had germinated ...

IV

The world spun round before the curate.

"Well, now I'm drunk," he said to himself. "What the devil – dammit! That's too much – that I couldn't exercise more self-control."

"The wine," the man of the house stammered, "wine is such a beast, the sort of beast – such a dangerous beast that, when we bite it, it ends up biting us ..."

He reached for his glass, but his hand was no longer master of its movements and tipped the glass over.

The lady saw that both men were completely sloshed and sneered disparagingly at them. She in fact enjoyed people when they were drunk. She'd witnessed her husband's drunkenness countless times and knew that it did him no harm. No matter how drunk he was, he could still put himself to bed. And she liked how, when he was drunk, he was entirely without concern. At such times he no longer cared about anyone or anything, he just talked and talked, even after he'd fallen asleep. And he said very strange things at those times. One could say that drunkenness brought him to his senses.

She also had plenty of occasion to see others while drunk, starting with her father when she was a little girl, and proceeding to perhaps every man she'd become acquainted with. She liked being the only sober person at the entire party. She enjoyed parties generally. And there was never a day when she didn't either have guests over to her place or go herself to parties where the men were drinking wine and courting women.

"No, it doesn't matter," the man of the house said, "it doesn't matter, just a little wine gone by the wayside ..."

"And my tablecloth!" the woman laughed.

"It's sad that a little wine was lost, but otherwise, no matter."

The curate saw what had happened, but he sat rigidly in his chair, not daring even to laugh. He knew himself and realized that if he were to move it would be all over for him. As long as he refrained from moving, no one would recognize that he was drunk, but if he were now to stand up, he would be overwhelmed by dizziness. He stared wide-eyed, gazing before him with the sternness of a professor at his lectern.

"So, you too are feeling fine," the lady said smiling.

"It doesn't matter," her husband said for the third time, "it's too bad that a bit of wine has been lost, but thank God there's plenty left in the Jew's cellar, thank God the Jew produces plenty in his cellar. Don't get wine from the cooperative, dear, since they sell real wine. It would have been a shame had real wine spilled. Pour me another."

"You're a fine bird. Every day you drink yourself merry, but look, the curate does no such thing."

"Real wine is no wine ..." the teacher repeated, letting his eyes close.

"Dear lady, you are a gorgeous woman!" the curate said, believing in his mind that he'd only thought the words.

"You don't say!" the lady laughed nervously.

"I am passionately in love with you, dear lady."

In that moment the teacher fell from his chair. He fell with great skill, as though his body were trained in such moves. His limbs accommodated themselves to the fall such that a smooth descent resulted. His wife had to laugh.

"Well, he's done for. Now I have to bring him to bed."

"It doesn't matter," the teacher mumbled, roused by his fall, "real wine is no wine. Forget it."

"Dear lady, you are more beautiful than any other woman."

"Do you even know what you're saying?"

"Of course I do, dear lady. You are more beautiful than any woman I've ever embraced."

"That can't be such a large assortment."

The curate grew silent and stared rigidly before him.

"Have you embraced a beautiful woman before, then?" the woman teased him.

"Yes. Dear lady, you are the most beautiful woman in the world!"

"You would be better off going to sleep."

The curate acted as though he understood what this meant.

"Of course now you don't know how you're to get to the hotel! It's no matter, I'll prepare a bed for you in the study. I'll call the student right away, he'll take you there."

The curate somehow sensed that the most beautiful woman in the world was disappearing before him, but it was no longer clear to him where to.

The lady was surprised not to find the student in his room. She called out softly from the window, then down the hallway. She didn't want to call out loudly, because another teacher's family lived on the ground floor, with whom they were on bad terms.

The student failed to appear, and she thought maybe he'd gone to visit some friend or other. But it was already past midnight ...

She returned to the front room where the curate remained seated in his chair, as though he hadn't moved an inch.

He made her laugh. "I must say, you're quite the hero," she remarked. "It might be a good idea for you to go to my nephew's room. Come, I'll take you there."

She walked over to the curate, but he just stared before him like a scalded fish.

"Come along, then."

No response.

"Just come along with me, sonny. That's it. Let's get up then ... All right ... that's it. And now forwards."

But of course the young man did not move forwards. He stood there, using his last bit of self-mastery to adopt oratorical poses. His face was rigid, as though he were sermonizing, and he stared forth in worshipful solemnity.

"That'll do ... Please, just come along with me."

With sudden decisiveness, she grabbed the young man around his back and forced him to start moving. He placed one foot in front of the other with the mechanical movements of a puppet.

They made their way out the door without incident.

In the middle of the hallway, the young man began to lurch and both of them nearly fell to the floor. Fortunately the wall was right there, and she managed to lean his limp body against it.

At this point the lady was afraid, she shook and perspired. She feared they might make noise.

"Laci!" she whispered.

Not a sound.

She placed her arm around the young man once more and led him further. Every step gave her joy, and she thanked God for each.

At last they succeeded in entering the room.

It was still empty – now there was no doubt that Laci was not at home.

"So, my child, so, just lie down like a good boy ... That's it, my little child ..."

She guided him to the bed.

In that moment the drunken man wrapped his arms around the lady's waist and brought her down onto the bed with him.

The woman was horrified. She couldn't breathe. "Let me go ..."

"You're the most beautiful woman in the world!" the young man breathed into her ear.

"Let me go! Let me go!" and with her nails she dug into the curate's flesh. But as though he couldn't even feel this, he slid his wine-tainted mouth back and forth across her face.

Her heart skipped a beat.

"Sweet girl!" the young man breathed ...

"Uneducated peasant!" the lady hissed. "I'm not a sweet girl! I'm not some restaurant cashier! I'm a gentlewoman! ..."

The youth didn't answer, as though he hadn't understood a word. He pressed his soft, hot face into the woman's cheek. With the full weight of his body, he pulled her down.

The lady could barely breathe under the strain. She'd worn herself out with dragging him in here and was too weak for such a collegiate beast. She grew limp, her strength failed her, and for a moment she ceased resisting.

She was seized in this moment by an awful pleasure. The young man's hand touched her. A giddy, torpid dizziness took hold of her and all the bitterness, every want she'd endured in her life, coursed through her, the blood rushed to her head and her resistance evaporated ... Not a soul was there ... Not a soul would know ... This, her accomplice, would not remember a thing ... Just one short moment later and she herself would not believe anything had happened.

... And now she could get satisfaction for all that fate had dealt her ... for all of it ...

This feeling lasted only a moment.

In the next moment she mustered all her strength and lifted the man off her so that he rolled against the wall, then she pulled herself together and lurched out of the room.

Her face burned red.

She had to stand in the openness of the vaulted corridor and breathe in lungfuls of the fresh, misty night air.

At last she collected herself and went into the front room.

There such a shocking, terrifying surprise greeted her that she could barely endure it.

Her husband was no longer lying beneath the table, the lamp was no longer in the room.

The door to the bedroom was open, and her husband lay in the bed, the lamp stood on the night table, and her husband slept snoring, having let his book fall onto the blanket, as though nothing had happened this evening ...

V

The next morning, the lady rose early. She saw as she got dressed that two buttons were missing from her skirt.

It disturbed her greatly to think she might have lost them during the scuffle.

She did not have a full-time servant at this time and generally subjected things to only superficial cleaning, but today she cleaned every nook and cranny with the greatest of care, reassuring herself that the two small buttons would turn up in the end.

Her husband now rose as well. He was just the same as after previous bouts of drinking, bleary-eyed, ill-humored, taciturn. In the courtyard below, the children who gathered in the early mornings were already buzzing about. It was a splendid, crystal-clear June morning; the fog of night had cleared out with the rising sun, sinking on the grass as tiny sparkling diamonds.

The lady shook out the dust cloth and stood there for a moment. She filled herself with the morning air.

"It's nice to get up early," she thought, and with a somewhat acrid smile she looked back into the front room where the strong smells of wine, stale smoke, and the night spent there hung irremovably.

She then went out into the kitchen to make breakfast. While the milk was cooking, she suddenly went out to the hallway and approached the student's door.

She opened it.

"Good morning, young men!"

Her nephew sat there at the table and was startled out of his half sleep. He sat as though he hadn't been to bed all night. His face sagged and he stared dully and listlessly before him.

The lady laughed and approached him motheringly with rustling steps. "What are you studying there, donkey?"

The student reached out with his two hands and covered something. Like when a person holds a butterfly, fearing that it will escape and fearing likewise that he'll damage it.

"So, what is that? Show me! ... Clearly you've had the lamp burning all night long. How I welcome such a prodigious waste of time! So what is it?"

With an obstinate glare, the youth refused to answer.

"I'm telling you to show it to me!"

The student fixed her with a stony stare from his sleep-deprived face and large, dark-encircled eyes, as though it didn't suffice to see this lady's face, rather he sought to see behind it, directly into her soul.

With the bravery of a child who dares to separate a lion from its prey, the lady placed her hand on the young man's.

"I must say, I'm very curious! Show me, Laci!"

She aimed a gaze at once pleading and cajoling at the youth's eyes, like an adult coaxing a child to give her something she can take from him with a simple motion of her fingers.

The young man's soul seemed to freeze, with large eyes and a heroic expression he looked the woman he at once despised and worshipped up and down several times over the course of a minute, then with grim decisiveness he stepped to the side. It was as though he'd summoned doom upon the woman's head with this movement.

Unfortunate soul! he said to himself and pitied the unhappy lady whose deed was thus laid bare ...

The lady recognized her buttons. Both of them lay there on the table. Beautiful little black buttons, with superb passamenterie, the intricate weblike weaving stretched tautly over a black silken base.

She turned up her mouth in derision, a deep wrinkle forming in one corner.

Then she turned away; she looked toward the bed. There lay the curate, his blanket drawn up to his ears, but fully awake. In motionless fear he watched what was taking place, without understanding. His sunken eyes glistened, and his expression was absurdly pathetic.

"Well, look at the hangover hero! How did you get to bed?"

The curate shrugged his shoulders and his little blond moustache drooped down over his mouth.

"Are you feeling poorly? Well?"

"Yes, sweet lady!" the young man said in his empty chest voice, then, as though a strange voice had met his ear, he began to reflect. The lady knew what he was thinking about; she turned and laughed.

"Just get dressed quickly, both of you, and come for breakfast."

She glanced once more at her little nephew and left the room.

The student followed her with his eyes and understood very little. In fact he understood nothing at all.

He began pacing back and forth across the room. With collegial familiarity, the curate spoke to him: "It would be good to sleep until noon."

Laci didn't answer; he began to undress. He tossed his jacket, vest and shirt to the side. He wanted to wash. He thought for a moment and started flexing and stretching his arm muscles. His arms were thin, he wasn't satisfied with them.

If only I were as strong as Pista Víg! he thought to himself. *Then I would tackle the curate and rip his soul from his body!*

The curate yawned and laughed out loud.

The student felt ashamed and blushed from one ear to the other. "Sorry bastard!" he grumbled. "At the very least someone should pour this basin full of water over his head."

The curate, too, jumped out of bed and began to dress.

The student looked enviously at the curate's long underpants which reached down to his ankles and buttoned at the waist, and it pained him that his own were like those of young boys, tied at the waist with a string and short, like swimming trunks ...

VI

The lady figured out everything. Laci had returned home, found the curate there on the bed, pitied him and gotten him out of his clothes. Beneath him he'd then discovered the buttons. And now he thought he knew everything.

This did not exactly make her happy, nor overly ashamed.

"Poor boy," she said to herself, "he didn't sleep all night long ..."

And now, too, she saw him seated at the table, leaning over the two buttons ...

She sensed how very, very much in love this little nephew was in her, and his sweet student's love pleased her.

She prepared some cocoa, brought it into the dining room, and called out as she passed through the hallway: "Gentlemen, hurry – time for breakfast!"

Hastily, she tidied up the room.

When she was finished, the young men gathered there. Her husband was the first to arrive. "So? Are the others still asleep? ..."

As the lady didn't respond, he continued: "Of course they are, the wretches. I'll just go and scare them out of bed."

He left the room.

The lady's face immediately curled into a spiteful sneer. She herself noticed the muscular movement in the corners of her lips and at first had to feel with her hand what it was. She thought some weight must be pressing on her there. "Ah, yes," she said, her sneer only growing more pronounced, "that's the heaviness of life weighing down on me."

Her husband returned momentarily with the curate.

The curate had washed himself up once again, combed himself, twirled his moustache up smartly, his clothes were clean, his cheeks rosy, only in his eyes could one detect that he hadn't gotten a proper night's sleep, and he struggled to resist yawning, suppressing the urge to the point that tears welled in his eyes from the effort.

"You conducted yourself nicely," the lady said to him and laughed to his face. A shared bout of drinking establishes a connection: it creates intimacy.

The young man blushed a little. "Don't be angry with me, gracious lady!"

"What on earth? … My, what a grand lady I've become!"

The curate lowered his eyes and a certain bewilderment colored his face. The lady observed him keenly … Did he remember something?

"Here we are," the teacher came with a large bottle in his hand, "a little Dutch courage for us. A clergyman needs his *spirits*!" He filled three glasses.

"Well now, let's see where your diploma has gotten you! Can you guess what this is?"

The curate lifted his glass, clinked it with the lady's, who looked into his eyes, whereupon the two of them smiled at each other.

He tasted the brandy. "Plum!"

"Of course!"

"Marc!"

"That would be something!"

He tasted it once again. "Juniper!"

The teacher laughed out loud. "Rosehip brandy!" he cried merrily. "Your smarts, my friend, are good only for the Bible!"

The curate polished off his glass. "Strong!" he said with a cough.

They sat down at the table. The student arrived, stealing silently, as was his wont, into his spot.

They ate, and until they'd cleaned their plates, no one spoke.

Then it seemed wise and good to each to get up and go to work ...

But something bothered the lady's conscience. "That was a nice get-together last night ..." And she turned to her husband: "How did you get to bed?"

The teacher stared helplessly. He couldn't remember.

The lady laughed. "I left you beneath the table, my dear. You were sleeping like a baby. And when I came in the bedroom, you were already in bed. The lamp was on the night stand and that nasty old newspaper was in your hand ..."

"I was reading?" the teacher asked intently.

"Of course not, you were sleeping and snoring like so much artillery ..."

"Excellent! Some things a man is completely unaware of! My friend," he said, turning to the curate, "I am possessed of the peculiar ability to make it into bed without assistance, no matter how drunk I am!"

"Not him, though!" the lady said, laughing at the curate.

"That's right, so how did you make it into bed?" the teacher asked him, his tongue slipping suddenly into the familiar "*te*" form of address.

The curate thought for a moment. He couldn't remember a thing. "I'm truly ashamed of myself."

"See here, friend," the teacher cried noisily, "a pig should be ashamed of itself, because it doesn't even drink wine, yet still ends up lying in the mud! A man has no need to feel ashamed! A man lies down from drinking wine! ... What one does under the influence is no cause for shame!"

The lady regarded her husband at length. She bit her upper lip and turned down the corners of her mouth in a disparaging grimace. The student looked at her with a fixed gaze from the end of the table.

The lady returned his gaze and laughed. "Ask Laci what you did," she teased him then. "Whether you've reason to be ashamed?"

All three of them looked at the student, whose face blushed flaming red. Even his eyes misted over.

"He carried you out," the lady went on, observing her nephew's face thoughtfully. "Poor Laci had to put up quite a struggle. He barely managed it. In the hallway he nearly dropped you. Fortunately he was able to lean against the wall and somehow managed to hold you up that way."

"Hahaha!" the teacher laughed, listening raptly to his wife's words. The curate did as well – though he was rather abashed, his curiosity concerning what followed was immense.

"It was marvelous," the lady continued, "when poor Laci, the poor man!" – and she all but stroked the student's face with her gaze – "when he said: 'What shall I do with him? ... What shall I do with him!'"

The two men laughed out loud, eyeing the student gleefully.

"But somehow he managed to get you into the room. I hadn't the faintest idea how to help him ..."

"Nor did I allow it," Laci said darkly.

" Of course he didn't! But my, did he struggle! Once he'd finally dragged you into the room, you, my fine curate, toppled over with your full weight, like an enormous sack, and pulled him down with you onto the bed."

The two men shook with laughter. The student grew pale.

The lady laughed and laughed. "It was all he could do to crawl out from under you," she said, "he slipped out from beneath you like a cat, gasping and hissing! Like a cat over which a basket has been placed."

The teacher and the curate crowed with laughter. The student lowered his head over his plate and scratched at the porcelain with his knife, producing a sharp scraping noise.

"Two buttons popped off of his suit as well ...," the lady reported once her laughter had subsided. "Right? That's why you changed your clothes?"

The student glanced up, only to look down again. During that first upward glance, a kind of uplifting feeling took hold of him. He sensed that the lady wanted to justify herself before him and he burned inside with happiness. But as he looked into his aunt's face, he saw such giddy, frivolous merriment there that he no longer dared to expect anything wonderful of her ...

"Well, that was excellent," the teacher and the curate agreed, wiping their eyes.

The curate regarded the student with increasing fondness, and spoke at last: "That's why you were so angry with me this morning! Please – he wanted to take it out on me and throw a bowl of water over my head!"

"Hahahahaha!" the teacher bellowed, unable to contain himself.

The student cast a haughty, disparaging glance at him.

The lady noticed this and looked warmly into his eyes, suddenly causing the youth's blood to boil giddily inside him. He leaned back in his chair and thought impulsively how splendid it would be to stand behind this woman's words, even were the earth to cave in on itself.

VII

The small, barefoot children produced a great uproar in the primary school when, towards noon, the caretaker opened the door. The teacher had no idea how to maintain discipline and the grammar school caretaker found the hellish noise unbearable.

He cast a magisterial glance at the restless herd of children and thought to himself: *This is why we have such a hard time with the grammar school students, because those primary teachers are educating the children so badly in their formative years.*

"Good morning, sir!" cried one of the children as he noticed that someone had entered the classroom. The others followed his example, droning forth the accustomed greeting.

The teacher looked over and motioned to the children to be quiet. No one of any consequence had entered, it was just the caretaker. "Yes? What is it?"

"If you please, teacher sir, the headmaster sends his regards and requests that you come and see him today. Right away, in fact."

"What for? What's the matter?"

The caretaker wrinkled his forehead with self-important secretiveness. "It has to do with the student Laci Veres ..."

The teacher looked at him for a moment in wonder, then nodded. "Good, I'll come. I'll be right there." He finished examining the third formers in geography, but was unable to focus on their responses.

Noon approached. He quickly issued instructions to his usual deputies, the capable older pupils, then left.

He went upstairs to his apartment, intending to have a word with his wife, but she wasn't there. He brushed off his clothes, took his other hat, grabbed his walking stick and left.

In the street he was greatly distracted. He was sorry not to have found his nephew at home. If only he could have asked him what had happened, whether he'd committed some act of foolishness or other.

In the street, he encountered Klein, the Jewish carter, who drove through the little town with such great self-respect, as though he'd leased the entire Koburg estate, even though it wasn't available for leasing.

"Good morning, teacher sir!" he greeted the teacher chummily.

Mr. Veres cringed. "Good morning ... How are you, Mr. Klein?"

"Fine."

As was his wont, the teacher proceeded to ask about his interlocutor's affairs. "Well, have you gotten everything settled with the magistrate? ..."

"There's no dealing with those skinflints. ... I'm not a Christian who donates his labor to the city! One load costs me seventy-five kreutzers, and they want to give me a crown. They'll just have to have someone else haul their wood ... I ask you, why should I finance this business out of my own pocket? That doesn't become a Jew." He laughed. His teeth shone black from his chubby face and he regarded the teacher with such a good-humored twinkle in his eye that Veres agreed with him.

"You're quite the man of action!" the teacher said, trying to speak in the manner of a carter.

"Tell me, what sort of a man is this new curate?" Klein asked in return.

"Oh, he's a magnificent lad!" the teacher replied, his eyes flashing, "a little green yet, but he'll do well. He had dinner at my place yesterday evening and got himself so drunk that my nephew had to drag him into bed."

"Why your nephew and not you yourself, teacher sir?"

"Because I, too, was inebriated!"

"So that's why! ..." They shook each other's hand, laughed, and took their leave in remarkably familiar fashion, as though having taken part together in a good-humored conspiracy.

The teacher left for the grammar school full of good cheer and thought about the drunken revelry of the previous evening. It amused him to know that the curate had had to be carried bodily into bed.

It wasn't until he found himself inside the great building that his heart sank a bit. Suddenly the feeling overcame him that he himself was a student being sent to the headmaster due to some mischievous prank or other.

He smiled at the thought.

What trivial matters those schoolboy pranks were when compared with the great pranks played by life!

Mysterious voices could be heard through the doors. The intermittently loud explanations of the professors, the students' responses ... He felt decidedly bad.

The headmaster sat in deep silence within his spacious office. As Veres entered, he knew for certain that he'd been summoned as the witness to some criminal proceeding or other. But he strived to smile and strode cheerfully across the long room.

The headmaster was perched behind his large, ornate desk. He directed the teacher to sit on the sofa off to his right, then continued to work on some writing task he could only complete by craning his neck like an egret.

When he was finished, he set his pen down carefully, glanced at the calendar, moved a few stacks of papers off to the side, and turned toward the teacher. "Esteemed colleague," he said, "where was your nephew last night?"

"Last night!" the teacher said with surprise, not daring to reciprocate the term "colleague." He feared that would express a certain superiority. "Last night? My nephew? He was at home. Naturally."

He fell silent. But the headmaster didn't respond. He didn't even look at him, he'd only cast a lightning-quick glance in his direction, in the true fashion of a "Lamb's Tail." Now the tall, pale, dark-haired man sat as though he were in the classroom behind his lectern, with a student standing before him who was about to earn a failing grade, as it was clear from the first word exiting his mouth that he had not prepared the day's assignment. It made no difference that he'd held the entire year's subject matter in the tip of his little finger, he could not answer the question now asked of him, and the headmaster took note of this with the well-known *schadenfreude* that always appears on professors' faces when they see what a gallows-worthy scoundrel the student is who does not possess absolute knowledge. There is something mysterious about a professor who, in situations concerning bad marks, occupies the same spiritual plain as the student and, setting all differences in regard to age, class, intellect, and life experiences aside, emerges as a simple fencing opponent who knows how to make use of his own individual tactics to ensure the student suffers defeat, assuming he's not simply stronger than he.

The teacher felt he was not prepared for today. He hesitated anxiously and stared before him, terrified, as though waiting for someone to rescue him with whispered answers. He cleared his throat weakly and continued: "The curate dined with me last night. The new curate!" His expression brightened somewhat, he believed this would cause every unpleasant feeling to vanish! "We had a nice little dinner! At around eleven o'clock, I said to my nephew, go now and attend to your studies ..."

He fell silent. It occurred to him that perhaps that had been around ten o'clock. Then he thought: *in case he needs an alibi* ... He regarded the headmaster, who was just staring absent-mindedly into space, behaving as he did when his student got stuck in the middle of a German translation exercise because he can't find the word he needs. He wouldn't help the poor soul for anything in the world. For minutes he waits, long, torturous minutes. Until the word eventually does come to him, at which point the lesson continues.

The teacher's forehead sweated profusely. "At around midnight, the curate began to grow weary ... He's a valiant lad, but the poor boy couldn't quite tolerate that bit of wine ..." – and he sensed the dissonance of this profane word spoken here in this room, where only temperance was taught and the boys were punished for the sake of temperance ... "Then my wife went out and called my nephew. And my nephew took the curate to his room and laid him there in bed ..."

Again he fell silent. "Why this particular question, if I may?" he asked then abruptly, for it was hardly appropriate that he be subjected to an interrogation like this.

"Well, if you please," the headmaster said with an acrid smile, "there is rather unfavorable news regarding the young man ... Yesterday evening at *a quarter past ten* he was seen on the street ... then he was seen on the street again, in tears, at *half past ten* ..."

"When?" the teacher asked, horrified.

"He said his aunt was ill ... Thank God, I looked into this today, and not a word of it is true ... And then he went to the students' apartment in Mrs. Pál Párdy's house and caroused together with the residents living there and registered here, and after midnight he left, but no one knows where he was until three o'clock, when he stole home ..."

"That's impossible!" the teacher exclaimed. He rose from his spot filled with horror, as though he were listening to a bloodcurdling witch's tale. "It's a lie!" he said, shaking his head.

Silence reigned again for a few moments. Anger boiled inside him then, and he said, infuriated: "It's truly horrifying how many shameless spies are lurking about the school! He should stand here before me, the person who saw that, so that I can spit in his face. At eleven o'clock Laci was still sitting in front of me, until that point he hadn't budged from the table. I sent him out to study at eleven o'clock."

The headmaster's face revealed nothing. "If you please, clocks can keep time very differently. According to *my watch*, it was precisely ten thirty when I encountered the graduand, László Veres, in the street ..."

The teacher was stunned. He sat back down and felt his world was coming to an end.

"The other facts are likewise completely trustworthy," the headmaster stated simply, as though the only difference of opinion between them concerned how their watches kept time.

They sat in silence for minutes on end. The teacher stared dumbly into space. By this point it wouldn't have surprised him to hear that his nephew had stolen chickens by night together with gypsies, been arrested by the gendarmes, sentenced to three months in jail, and nevertheless shown up at breakfast this morning, as though nothing whatsoever had happened.

He no longer dared look at the headmaster and sensed in his face that, the moment he lowered his eyes, the headmaster regarded him so intensely that his gaze singed his skin. He returned the gaze in spite of himself and saw how in that moment the headmaster turned his eyes away from him. But the moment his eyes strayed away again, he immediately felt the other's suspicious, searching, cunning gaze.

Neither spoke a word for an unbearable length of time.

Then someone entered the room.

It was Hounddog, the professor. The entire town knew him by this moniker, the students' nickname for him being highly appropriate.

The professor approached with a sallow smile. His face revealed the respect due the headmaster as well as the ease resulting from a certain chummy intimacy; the intense indignation inspired by Laci Veres's crime alongside his pity for the unfortunate uncle. It revealed his sorrow regarding the depravity of today's youth as well as his comforting sense of his own steadfast integrity. All this was found in his long, pale face, in the watery, bulging eyes, which looked as though they wanted to jump out across his large, shiny glasses.

There, in the way he shook hands, barely touching that of the teacher as he reached out for it briefly while recognizing the headmaster with a silent bow, he indicated that, although he had only just now entered the room, he respected the headmaster as a man, as an educator, as a proper grammar school director, as well as a merciless investigative judge and verdict pronouncer in today's deplorable criminal matter.

The professor leaned against the headmaster's desk and rested his left elbow on the shelf holding his documents. "Shocking!" he said simply, and shook his head.

"But if I may," said Veres, "I don't really know what happened. Did my nephew commit some sort of offense?"

Hounddog looked at the headmaster in wonder, as though he wanted to ask what the deuce those barbarous parents were after. He perceived how the headmaster entrusted him with conveying the bearings of the case, so to oblige him he addressed himself to the teacher in a brusque, accusatory fashion: "If you please, the boy committed such heinous acts during the night that, in the interest of the school's good name, it's necessary to settle everything with utter thoroughness ... Last night at ten o'clock he left the building and didn't return until three in the morning. In particular, there is no information regarding where he was from two until three o'clock after midnight."

He removed a notebook from his pocket. The words, written in splendid gold lettering: "Professors' Handbook," shimmered on the cover. He paged through the entire book. At the beginning all his students' names were entered, and he smirked as he glanced briefly over the countless grades entered next to them. His attention was especially captivated by the overly large "D's" recorded there. Had time allowed his brain to come up with a thought of any kind, occupied as it was with the feverish disentanglement of the great event, he would certainly have remarked how sad it was that today's students showed so little devotion to learning Latin and Greek. This vast number of D's served as proof. He then paged further and took note of the ministerial decrees and new ordinances recorded there. This section raised his self-esteem significantly, as this rubric of his notebook made him an impressive authority at the instructor conferences: he had precise knowledge of the most detailed questions concerning the will of the minister. Following this were the titles of new publications in the field of classical philology and the names of their publishers. These he noted with the goal of conducting a neverending, futile war with the librarian over the acquisition of these books for the school library. As the annual allowance for the library was quite small – it amounted to barely 150 forints – and acquisition of the expensive French and English critical editions was out of the question, the librarian made a habit of arguing in these disputes that none of the professors, especially the classical philologists, understood French or English, but this was obviously a totally absurd argument, since a proper expert, when it comes to growing and perfecting the library collection, never has his own egotistical goals in mind, but always the absolute needs of the library! And how could one imagine a halfway decent classical philology collection without the London Malthers edition, which included all Latin and Greek authors with the only complete textual critique and all notations that had been made over two millenia regarding the authors in question! It was deplorable that the Hungarian philological treatises were unknown to this otherwise excellent publisher, so that the doctoral dissertation of Professor Hounddog was not included in the Cicero commentaries, even though precisely the Cicero edition was in need of supplementation, as Cicero consisted merely of 70 volumes in the Malthers edition. My God, what satisfaction it would have meant to the professors of the Budapest faculty if the edition had included this treatise: the professors in Pest had in fact not accepted it as a basis for the doctorate, and as a result these two coveted letters are lacking in front of his name to this day, and the printing of his dissertation had cost him, in spite of the reduced charges of the local printing house, twenty-six forints per sheet.

Unfortunately, he now jumped over a significant portion of the notebook so I can't state what all else was to be found in this rich book. A great deal was there, as we are at the end of the school year, and a professor can record all that happens over the course of an entire year in only a single notebook.

On the page that stood open, the register of the students' offenses was located. After a raft of names, he found the page on which the following was written:

> I. *Veres, László*, student, 8th
> form
> June 7, 1910, 10:17 p.m., on
> corner of ave.: goes to
> Gacsal's, who'd requested
> Lat. vocab. from him, as was

likewise preparing Latin
exam. Untrue.
10:35 p.m. Headmaster
encounters him on ave.
bridge. Crying. Aunt is ill.
Emphysema. A lie.
10:30 p.m. – 1:30 a.m. at
István Víg's with roommates.
Revelry.
1:30-3 a.m. – where?

All this was written in tiny letters, with some of the words abbreviated so as to make room for more. One must use the pages of the notebook sparingly, as there was only one more clean sheet after this one, and who knew how many more students' names would have to fit there!

"If you please, everything is written here. Only one point isn't clear to us: where was the lad between half past one and three o'clock?"

The teacher rubbed his forehead. What was it that his wife had said, how Laci had gotten the curate into bed. If he wasn't at home ... But the curate had stated the same thing ... Ugh – he can't remember a thing. But then someone must have lied, either the boy or the wife ... That couldn't have been a lie! The woman even laughed at how the curate fell onto Laci and how two buttons popped off of his jacket. That's why he'd changed clothes.

"If you please, I know nothing. I got myself a bit drunk last night, the curate was there, the new curate, he dined at our place, we both tied one on ... we felt very good!"

"Scandalous!" the professor said, "and the vile lad took advantage of the opportunity and absconded ..."

The teacher moodily rubbed his forehead once again. "But please, tell me, did my nephew do something, then? Something shameful? Did he harm someone? Did he do something bad?"

"My dear colleague," the headmaster put in, and he stretched forth his head as though he were inserting it into a yoke. His large Adam's apple rose and fell. "After all, you, too, are an instructor! You understand the goals of education. This sort of disciplinary misstep, and precisely in the midst of the most disagreeable time ... directly before the exams, cannot be tolerated!"

The professor nodded in approval at the headmaster's words, and when he saw that the man did not continue his speech, he took over: "We must hold these young students to strict disciplinary standards, for their own good. What would happen if we were to loosen the reins on them? In that case we would be in the same position as that we read about in the papers concerning the schools in Brazil, where the students simply gun down their professors from off their podiums." He straightened his pince nez and chuckled. Then he sensed that this jest was out of place and would not be appreciated by the headmaster. So he made a serious face and proceeded to subject the necessity of disciplining today's youth and the damaging effect of poor examples to scientific analysis.

But the teacher no longer had ears for his words, as he was absorbed in contemplation of how somebody must have been lying. Either these two here were lying, or the two at home were.

He stood up. "If I may, I agree it's necessary to teach our youth the importance of an orderly life, but please, I still don't know if my nephew has done anything or not."

The headmaster and the professor looked at him disconcertedly. "Was the lad at home last night or not?" Hounddog asked with professorial sternness.

"Well if we must, let's say he wasn't at home."

"He wasn't at home! And where was he then this morning between two and three o'clock? This, I contend, constitutes a serious disciplinary lapse ..."

In this moment, the caretaker appeared. "Mr. Headmaster, sir, I humbly report that the student László Veres is here."

"Have him come in."

A minute passed and Laci entered. He was pale and shaking. He stood as though about to be condemned to death.

He was taken aback to see his uncle, who stared at him wordlessly, likewise filled with anxiety. The unexpected encounter took them both by surprise.

Silence reigned for several minutes.

"My son, I called you here so that you might relate everything regarding this unpleasant and unusual affair that has taken place."

The boy said nothing. Intense nervousness was drawn in his pale face and the dark shadows under his eyes. His uncle noticed for the first time how thickly the boy's moustache was growing in.

Then the professor began in a cloying tone: "Dear boy, let's just discuss everything as good friends. So, yesterday evening you left the building ... That's fine. Your kindly uncle told us what happened ... at least as far as he knows ..."

The headmaster interrupted him. It bothered him that this overzealous underling might lie in his presence. "Until when did the dinner last?"

The student looked at him without answering.

"Answer me! Until ten or eleven? Ten, right?"

Laci said nothing.

"Until ten, then. Some incidental detail had your uncle confused, or perhaps the clock at home is off, given that he recalls it lasted until eleven ..."

He fell silent, waiting for confirmation. The boy said nothing.

"Until ten, then. At that point, you went to your room. What did you do there? Nothing?"

The boy stood mutely. He looked down at the ground.

"Nothing, then. Why did you leave the building? You told the professor you were going to Gacsal's for the vocabulary notebook. Since Gacsal is also working on the Latin assignment ... You see? Already you're feeling ashamed. It's even easier to catch a liar than to catch a lame dog. Even then it was clear to the professor that something wasn't right! For he was just coming from Mr. Robert Gacsal's home, where they were celebrating Robert's name day. And there he spoke with your friend, who admitted that he hadn't yet done the Latin assignment, as this honest, upstanding boy is incapable of lying ... And what did you say to me? That your aunt was ill. I visited with her this very day. She was on her way to church this morning in the peak of health, just as I was arriving at the school ... And then how did it enter your mind to go to Víg's room, where you'd never been before ... How can a young man fall so abruptly into iniquity? ... Don't you love your parents? Those poor people who can hardly wait to see their son become an independent person, whom they have raised up at tremendous cost to themselves ... Isn't that right, Mr. Veres?"

The teacher gave a start. He stared fixedly at his nephew, at his determined, stubborn face.

He looked at him as though he'd never seen this face in his entire life. As though he merely bore striking resemblance to some acquaintance of his ...

His nephew seemed tall and grown up to him, yet when he tried to recall him in his memory, he only saw a small, smiling, quiet child, who wore knickers over his skinny legs and carried a big load of books bundled together with a strap on his way to school. He was prone to laughing at him and constantly teased him when he came home: "Tell me, my little pupil: Did you respond? ... or merely despond?"

And now this lanky youth seemed so foreign to him, as though he meant nothing to him. His moustache was sprouting ... His huge, red fists quivered, and obduracy and defiance shone on his face.

A word from the headmaster startled him. He had no idea what he was talking about.

"Speak up, boy ... Look on us as your parents' deputies. See your uncle here. An honest, educated man, beyond reproach, whom everyone loves, everyone honors, and with whom we, his colleagues, entertain the friendliest of relations. I can truly tell you that you have him to thank for our willingness to handle this matter in such a lenient, informal manner ... Tell us where you were from two until three in the morning."

The young man's face suddenly flinched. His forehead turned red. But he lowered his head even more and maintained his silence.

"Speak, my boy, speak!" the headmaster said somewhat angrily.

But Laci didn't say a word — they waited in vain.

The teacher's ire began to rise. "Well, why don't you answer?" he demanded of his nephew.

The boy raised his head and looked his uncle in the eye. His gaze was moist, clouded, nothing could be read from it.

"Where were you last night?"

Laci looked at his uncle for another moment, then silently lowered his eyes, as a repressed sigh exited his chest.

Hounddog adjusted his pince nez, replacing its gold chain behind his ear, as it had worked its way loose in his agitation. Then he spoke in a honeyed voice: "My dear boy, speak to us with the same degree of intimacy that a child confesses everything to his own mother."

Laci's look darkened and he called to mind that sad summer, that unbearable and desolate home where he could no longer confess a single thing to his mother, whom he loved above all else in the world.

"Were you at home yesterday or not? ... Did you bring the curate into bed? What!" the teacher yelled. "I'll teach you!"

"Shh," the headmaster said.

"Nothing doing — the cur will talk, or I'll break every bone in his body!" Veres yelled again. "What, young man? I had you go study! Everything was fine! And now you bring such shame on me! Where were you loitering about?

Swine! You sneak away from home and traipse around God knows where."

The small man jumped agitatedly from one foot to the other. His face flared red and his long moustache drooped completely across the black opening of his mouth.

Laci made a sad face; he looked ill.

"Just leave matters to me!" the teacher screamed. "I'll squeeze the answer out of him!" And he stepped in front of the youth, grabbed him by the collar, and forced him to raise his head and look him in the eye.

"Well? Speak! Speak then! ... Did you bring the curate to his room? Did you put him into bed?"

It was evident from the young man's face that he wanted to speak. He made such a decisive step backwards that his uncle let him go. "Yes, of course, I put the curate into bed."

"So? And where were you till three o'clock?" Hounddog asked with his head tossed back.

"At home in my bed!"

"Liar!"

"I don't lie."

"You don't?! ... Last night to me you did! You said your vocabulary notebook was at Gacsal's!"

"I did not."

"No?! I met you in the street at seventeen minutes after ten" – and he grabbed his notebook hastily, having written it down there.

"You didn't meet me in the street, sir."

The professor was stunned – his pince nez tumbled off his nose as shock took hold of him. "I didn't meet you in the street?"

"No. Not me!"

The headmaster stood abruptly. He stared at the youth with grim, blood-freezing sternness. "You didn't meet me either?"

"No, headmaster, sir."

The room was grave-still.

The youth eyed first the one man, then the other with courageous calm. He didn't lower his eyes, in fact the impact of his words seemed almost to amuse him. "When my uncle said I should go to bed, I drank one last glass of wine at the table with them, then I went to my room and spent the rest of the evening studying Horace. After midnight, I don't know exactly what time it was, my aunt came and told me to come to her right away, so I went into the front room. There lay the curate drunk on the floor, as he'd fallen from his chair, and next to him lay my uncle, his head under the table as he, too, had fallen from his chair, and he lay there like a small child. I lifted the curate and carried him out, it was very difficult when I tried to get him onto the bed, and when I tried to lay him down there I slipped onto the bed and he fell on top of me. He weighed heavily on me, as when one is rather weak it's hard to slither out from beneath such an ox without being crushed," he said softly. Then suddenly: "But I managed to crawl out!" he yelled, then continued with a fiery tone: "I summoned every scrap of strength and squeezed myself out from under him. My jacket was buttoned and in my struggle two buttons popped off. Those two buttons."

The teacher heard all this as if in a dream. He looked at the buttons, the missing buttons, and a strange bewilderment took hold of him. Those two buttons! His wife had also mentioned them, the two missing buttons!

"Shocking! Never in my teaching career has such a case ever occurred before!" said Hounddog: "That someone could lie this way!"

"If you please, professor sir, I'm not lying."

"Repeat it once again: Did you meet me in the street or not?"

"I didn't meet you in the street."

"And you weren't in Víg's room, either?"

"I've never been there in my life."

"And if I read off the names of the other ten students, if I call each of them here, you still weren't there?"

"No."

"You spent the entire night at home and slept peacefully."

"Yes."

"I hereby give you notice that you should, from this moment on, regard yourself as barred from attendance at any school in the entire country."

Frightful silence.

"Only by means of the most contrite confession can you repair the damage ..."

Silence.

"You may go."

The youth turned around and left with confident, calm steps.

The three men regarded each other. In his bewilderment, Hounddog removed his pince nez and began to clean it. When he was finished, he looked through it, blinking into the light. The headmaster worked to control his expression. He sought to remain stone-hard. This minute, in which he had initially sensed such self-satisfaction, had shocked him to his core – he feared he might have miscalculated and encroached on the sphere of God's power.

He would have been very glad had some miracle come to his aid and undone everything that had just happened, had the student returned tearfully to beg for forgiveness and all could be resolved with a short term of detention ...

But they waited in vain, the student did not return. He rang for the caretaker. "Send László Veres back here."

"Yes, headmaster sir, I'll run after him. He left."

"He left?"

"Yes, sir."

The headmaster indicated that he should let it go and be on his way. Then he looked wanly at the teacher. Now, confronted with the great task, his energy was depleted, though he could certainly be pitiless when it came to a student's inadequate classroom performance. Now he simply waxed loquacious, as though he were to blame for everything and sought at this point to wash himself clean.

"It's absolutely astonishing what's become of this boy. Never has there been any reason to complain about him. From a moral standpoint his behavior has always been blameless."

"And now too, he's telling the truth," the teacher said, "those two buttons! It's not possible to make up such a thing!"

"Please, I met him in the street! Spoke to him then just as I am to you now! And I was shocked. He was crying! Why was he crying? Such a grown lad! There must have been a reason! Graduands aren't accustomed to crying! It's inconceivable! Inconceivable! ..."

He turned then and said apprehensively: "Now I am forced to bring the matter before the faculty council. Terrible, terrible."

A strident ringing sound caused them to start. All three of them winced in fright, yet it was only the bell signalling the end of the class period.

At that point they felt as though a particularly grueling class session had reached its end. They breathed a sigh of relief, then shook hands as they took leave of each other.

The headmaster returned to his seat, the professor left with the teacher and returned to the faculty room. The teacher, for his part, descended the stairs, his head reeling.

The classrooms opened, one after the other, and as the professors exited them, an infernal din took over the school. Mr. Veres stood amidst the thundering herd of homeward bound students, as though caught in a stampede as the swarm of students in every shape and size swept past him.

Once he reached the street, he heaved a great sigh. He removed his hat from his head and wiped the sweat from his forehead.

In that moment someone tapped him on the shoulder: "Good morning, Mr. Bovary!"

The teacher turned around. It was the deputy judge.

Then he had the idea of telling everything to this legal expert. He understands such matters and would tell him the truth.

And immediately he felt good again, as though he'd found a safe asylum in the midst of the earth's destruction.

VIII

He didn't dare give voice to the idea that had occurred to him. He felt this wasn't the appropriate time to rush and reciprocate the judge's uncomfortable intimacy with his trust. A vague suspicion told him that this strange monicker was intended as an insult.

So he continued walking along and found it odd that, at a time when such great and bitter troubles afflicted him, he should accompany this gentleman with such good-humored calm, as though nothing had happened to him, to his nephew, or his wife.

The deputy judge knocked his cane cheerfully against the cobblestones and then, tired at last of the protracted silence, commented: "So this is the famous pavement? ... Splendid, how Uncle Berta brags about there being no similar pavement anywhere else in the county!"

Uncle Berta was the mayor. Actually it was Uncle Berti, but he entertained such good relations, admittedly platonic relations, with little Berta from the large inn, that the entire town, even the newly arrived deputy judge, jokingly called him Uncle Berta behind his back. The young man smiled as he called the short, dumpy mayor to mind, who often sat boasting at the long tavern table beside his spritzer; imitating Berti's voice he continued: "I'm the one who made something of Ilosva! ... I've done it all here ... Wasn't it I who introduced electric lights here? ... Nowhere in the county do they have the pavement we have here! ..." And in his natural voice the judge added: "Well, in the countryside, every town already has asphalt!"

The teacher felt the need to defend his town. "Certainly, because in the countryside there aren't any stones! There stones would cost more than asphalt. But our trachyte, the Ilosva trachyte, is famous across the country."

"In any case, Uncle Berta could have cut the sidewalk wider," the deputy judge said disparagingly, "as long as he made it."

"What has that old ass ever made!" the teacher reacted, using a far coarser term than was his custom. "The man does nothing, he just sits around thinking up schemes and pursuing his own sleazy ends."

He furrowed his brow crossly and began to twirl his thick moustache with a vengeance. He was overcome by the need to curse. It made perfect sense that now, with his head full of his own problems, with what the papers would call a "bullet in his flesh," in the precise moment when he brooded over how he could be discussing the greatest unpleasantness of his life with this man, they had to argue about the pavement ...

The deputy judge smiled. He felt it strange to breathe in the air of these small town rivalries. Life-and-death battles emerged among people over these petty town affairs ... To him, who stood at a great distance from them, from the entire town, in terms of his objective detachment, these disputes were as alien as the life of ants. He refrained from speaking as he sensed that the teacher saw in him one of the mayor's supporters, and that his fulmination was also directed at him. For some reason he didn't want to seem unsympathetic toward the spunky little man; only later did the thought of his wife occur to him.

They walked along in silence.

The teacher also decided it was a bad idea to ruffle the judge's feathers as long as he had it in mind to ask him for advice. So he thought better of it.

He stopped and pointed at a long, low building on the opposite side of the street that was filled with little shops. Long-bearded Jews stood before the doors, merrily smoking their pipes; from time to time a syllable or two of their odd German mumbling reached their ears, and odors of every kind emanated almost visibly from the dark, low-built doors that resembled the squat entrances to so many mines – in fact there was indeed a gold mine amongst the thousands of wares filling all the nooks and crannies here. Behind this building stood a large, plain, yellow, two-story edifice whose upper-floor windows peeked out over the roof of the first building, as though seeking to stand on tiptoe and peer across the square, where arrestingly interesting sights might meet the eye ...

"If I may," the teacher said, "please have a look at this building. Wouldn't it be great to simply tear down this heap of rubble and build an imposing, beautiful, modern edifice in its place, with large windows, decorations of majolica, just like in Pest! Wouldn't that be wonderful!"

"Yes. That would be nice."

"It would give the entire town a new face. It would make a modern city of this tired old nest! Based on the contract with the state, this is where the new primary school ought to be erected! A building that would provide housing for three teachers! A modern building! With balconies! ... for the director, for me, and for Dvihally. You should know, that is what the mayor has blocked."

He gave the deputy judge an important look, but the judge only smiled, and Veres felt that this young, unmarried man now regarded him as egotistical.

Somewhat bewildered, he continued: "Please don't think that I've lost anything by this, rather the town has. I mean, what greater ideal could one conceive of than a primary school on this spot! The large building behind there is the agricultural school which the state is renting from the town. Between them would be a beautiful playground. A veritable paradise! There wouldn't be a more magnificent campus anywhere else in the county ..."

He shook his head bitterly.

"And just think now what sort of man the mayor is! He's also the church trustee, so he made it his main goal to free the church from its obligation to maintain the primary school. The school was transferred to the state. That was all well and good, we were glad as we thought that everything would be fine now. Well, at least we became employees of the state. The state drew up a contract whereby it took over all costs associated with the school, but the city is obligated to erect a nice palace for it in place of this ramshackle shanty."

He waved his hand despondently, then reached into his inner pocket from whence he retrieved a lonely, somewhat careworn, wrapped cigar. He corrected its faults with a lick here and there, then continued his speech: "But the mayor has got it into his head now that he should also free the town from the burden of the primary school. I ask you, what has this man schemed up with his peasant's brain, his cobbler's imagination! I'll tell you, he's figured out, first of all, that if they build the palace it will cost a lot of money, and secondly that the city will lose the rent from these shops! So suddenly he comes forward with how the agricultural school, the state school here, is large and poorly suited, as it lacks a garden. Thus the town should take it back and use it to house the primary school. The state, for its part, should get a nice piece of land at no cost where it can build the sort of school it wants, complete with a garden to its liking. And would you like to know what sort of land he would have the town give the state for the school? ... The old cemetery!"

"Splendid!" the deputy judge burst out.

"Yes, dear sir, they're saddling those long-dead people with the entire public education system."

The deputy judge laughed out loud.

The teacher noticed that some professors were coming up behind them and rushed ahead, as he didn't want to meet up with them. His great worries likewise entered his mind, and with that he ceased to be troubled by the town's problems. He rubbed his eyes, then lit his cigar with a match.

"So, you aren't using a lighter, teacher sir?" the judge asked.

"Oh, I totally forgot that I have one," Veres responded. "It's just easier the old-fashioned way, with a match."

The deputy judge smiled.

On the other side of the street, the butcher stood outside his shop. His arms were crossed over his chest and his filthy, bloody apron was bunched up inside his belt.

"There's much that is interesting going on in this little town," the deputy judge said, "and yet also a frightful amount of the commonplace. I mean, isn't it boring that this brave butcher has to look exactly like butchers are portrayed in any satirical magazine. As though he'd crawled directly out of the oldest pages of Munich's *Fliegende Blätter* humor rag. Fat, pot-bellied, tuber-nosed – one grows weary of life when one sees how nature no longer brings forth anything, not a single thing one could label original ..."

"But please," the teacher spoke, "this man is no fool. During the parson election in spring, before you arrived here, Mr. Horácsek" – with this he waved across the street to the butcher – "paid for three barrels of wine for Tanner Street so that they would vote not for the new parson, but for the old one we're currently stuck with."

"Is that so!"

"Because he has a son who's a theologian and can't yet become a parson. Brave Uncle Horácsek here didn't want to see a young parson selected who would live for another fifty years, since such a man couldn't be given the sack willy-nilly. After all, his son should return here to be parson when the time comes! So, if you please, he studied each candidate one by one and determined who was most appropriate! This old man struck him as the best! He'll last just long enough for his son to be eligible for election. Then he can pass peacefully into Abraham's arms."

He laughed at this with his rotten teeth, while the deputy judge guffawed and thought to himself what a delightfully dear, pleasant man the teacher was.

"But he if keeps on living! There's no way to know how long a man will live."

"As if! It's his stock and trade, he's been working with beasts his entire life long."

They arrived at the large inn laughing merrily.

"Well, wouldn't you like to partake in a glass of beer inside?" the deputy judge asked.

"Not a bad idea before a meal!" the teacher replied. "I'd like to ask your judiciary advice in a certain matter in any case."

"Of course, I'm at your disposal."

They went inside and within ten minutes the teacher had told him everything.

IX

The teacher was unhappy with his account. He couldn't warm up to the topic and felt like everyday life had now drowned this extraordinary and dreadful event in a filthy flood of muck. After his halting delivery he sensed that the whole story had evolved into a run-of-the-mill, small-town sensation similar to ones he'd told before ... He felt ashamed and saw now that he shouldn't have indulged in his jabbering earlier. Whoever has truly been struck by disaster cannot afford to waste his breath on gossip!

He bit his lip and tugged on his moustache. He shot the deputy judge a nervous look.

The young man was silent. He gazed before him immersed in thought, a preoccupied look on his face, occasionally tapping the ash from his cigar. He'd regretted for some time now living in this little town of which he'd already formed the strangest impression and heard tales that made his eyes bulge in wonder without conjuring up a single clear picture. He lived here like a man who carries a gun under his arm as he wanders across the most famed of hunting grounds, encountering Sunday hunters who were downing beautiful and exotic specimens left and right, while he himself failed to take aim at so much as a skinny rabbit. He surpressed his excitement, fearing that he could scare off his prey that stood there with nervous ears, suspecting the presence of a hunting dog, with a single small movement.

This time he would not let the quarry escape his range. He called to mind the image of the teacher's beautiful little wife who had occupied his fantasy throughout the entire evening, this true small-town paradigm who thanked God that the piglets had croaked ... And in a completely natural tone, he said: "Dear Mr. Bovary ..."

He stopped, hesitated, anxious not to scare off his prey before he got in close enough range to take aim at it ...

The teacher looked up at him in astonishment. "Please, my name is Veres, Pál Veres."

"Sorry," and he placed his hand considerately on the teacher's arm and flashed a dismissive smile, "it's nothing ... That name is sort of an *idée fixe* of mine. It means nothing ... Rest assured, I have a clear understanding of the matter. It's just that I can't make a statement until I've seen all the players with my own eyes. My dear sir, you were kind enough to invite me yesterday evening ... I think for dinner tomorrow? Is the invitation still in force?"

"Why of course ..."

"In that case, don't speak of this matter to anyone until then. There's absolutely no point in making it public ... Indeed, I would prefer that no one, not a single person in the entire town, learn a word of this before tomorrow evening ..."

"Of course ... I won't tell a soul ..."

"In the interests of the investigation. You know it must be this way with any inquiry. And then just stay calm. A man must be philosophical."

The deputy judge furrowed his brow and settled back down in his seat. In this moment he merely played the role of philosopher ... He remained convinced that the wife had given herself over to the curate during the night, that the student knew this, and now wanted to sacrifice himself! That was the simplest hypothesis, as nothing else would involve the woman having compromised herself. And the assumption that held the most water was that the woman had done something scandalous ...

The teacher clinked glasses with the judge and they drank up their beers.

"Well, I'll be on my way then," Veres said, setting down his glass.

"Hello, Pali!" Dvihally called to him from behind, having just entered the room.

The teacher looked at him in surprise and rushed over to his friend.

"Antal Dvihally, my colleague and friend," he introduced the man to the deputy judge with a smile, unable to call the latter's name to mind. The deputy judge reached out his hand and smiled.

"Ah, the deputy judge," Dvihally said, "very happy to meet you."

They bowed to one another and helplessly avoided eye contact for a moment.

"So, friend, have a seat," Veres said to Dvihally, who was clearly burdened by something, but he sat down just the same.

"A glass of beer before lunch is no bad thing," he remarked by way of saying something innocuous.

Little Berta quickly brought them three glasses of beer.

At the neighboring table sat several town dignitaries, at the next the judges and attorneys. The company conversed noisily, everyone spoke across his own table to his neighbor's too, as it was more or less coincidence that had determined who gathered at which table. Everyone was either already eating or had just ordered and was waiting for his meal to arrive. When they had been two, the deputy judge hadn't wanted to eat, but now he called over the waiter and ordered soup.

Getting their conversation going proved difficult. The deputy judge, like Veres, was immersed in thought. Dvihally was a taciturn man who only spoke if something piqued his interest.

"What's the matter, old man?" Veres asked him.

"Nothing's the matter," Dvihally replied, and he rubbed both temples simultaneously with his long, bony fingers. "But what is going on with your nephew? Are they throwing him out of school or what the hell!"

The teacher and deputy judge looked at him in wonder, even shock.

"Where do you know that from?" Veres asked anxiously.

"Zimmer said it earlier in the street ..."

"Zimmer! Which one?"

"The carpenter."

"Where does he know it from?"

"I don't know, but he said that they called your nephew in today to tell him he was being expelled. And reportedly they called you in as well, so they could tell him in your presence! ... I don't know what's true and what's not, but three or so of the people here heard it as well."

"So what have you to say about that!" Veres asked the deputy judge. "Try to keep something secret here. How does one of the Zimmers know about my affairs! Something happened one short hour ago, and now the entire town knows about it."

"Please, this is a huge affair! Expelling someone before his final examinations! We must be dealing with an enormous blunder on the professors' part! I was just saying, I know your nephew, it's simply impossible, he's the last person who ..."

"Most unpleasant!" the deputy judge said.

"So the deputy judge already knows it as well!" Dvihally remarked in amazement.

The deputy judge smiled moodily without responding.

"So then there really is something to it!"

More people entered the tavern. After a time, a young man with a limp rose from some table across the room, came up to Veres and asked him in a low voice: "Please, teacher sir, is it true what they're saying about your nephew?"

"Why?" Veres asked, turning toward him with reddened eyes.

"Because I ran into Laci yesterday evening. That is, it was already this morning. He was down in the city garden, sitting there on a bench, and he said he'd already been there an hour. We'd been out amusing ourselves, so I went home late. I asked him what he was doing there. He talked about this and that, said he was mulling over some philosophical question. What do I know – I really didn't understand much, as I was rather tipsy. But I understood enough to be amazed by what he said, and I thought to myself, a great man will emerge one day from this youth! And please, what nonsense to think he'd gone to *Master Street*! Not a young man like him! Those assinine professors absolutely don't understand such young people! Expelling him from school! I mean please, if they do that, then by God they should beat the living daylights out of that filthy Hounddog!"

"I know nothing about any of this!" Veres said, glancing with half-closed eyes at his two companions, who listened raptly to the young man's hushed talk.

"But that's shocking! You know absolutely nothing!" the young man cried. "Monstrous, this veritable rat's nest of gossip! There's no doubt about it, people should avoid Ilosva like the plague, there's no worse gossip mill in all of Hungary! Please, gentlemen, I beg you to excuse me."

"Who is that young man?" the deputy judge asked.

"I don't know," Veres responded, "I've never spoken to him before in my life." He blinked his eyes repeatedly and scratched himself on the chin. He sat there like a frightened dog.

"It's certainly true," Dvihally remarked, "here everyone lives for gossip."

"What should I do now?" the teacher turned suddenly to the deputy judge.

"I really don't know. It's important to act quickly. I can no longer wait until tomorrow evening."

"I've asked the deputy judge to uncover the truth," Veres reported to Dvihally, whereupon an idea occurred to him. "Please, judge sir, come over to my place for dinner!"

"I simply couldn't ..."

"Of course you could, we're used to it. It's hardly the first time I've brought an unexpected guest home to my wife ... Nor is it the last," he added with a flash of amusement. "Waitress, check please!"

The deputy judge hesitated. "I haven't even been introduced to your wife yet!"

"Then I will introduce you!" the teacher said with a smile.

"Good, then. I'm conducting an investigation, in that case anything goes! The most important thing is speed!"

"Let's go, then. My, but the waitress is taking her time! Oh well, we'll pay later on ... Good-bye! Farewell, my friend, good day."

They took leave of the noisy company right and left and made their exit.

X

This time the lady was quite angry over her husband's bringing a guest home so unexpectedly. She had no meat available for dinner and the other foods had been cooking too long now, they'd lost their flavor. She asked the day maid to go to the butcher shop, and the maid herself cursed and raved in the kitchen until her anger was exhausted.

Had the situation been different, the deputy judge would have felt very awkward, but as it was he smiled to observe how the man of the house walked about with that sheepish expression peculiar to husbands whose wives are in a grumpy mood, while the guest is not supposed to notice anything.

The wife thought it over and finally entered the room.

"Play some piano, dear," the teacher said.

The lady obliged and went over to the piano. "As if one could play on this instrument," she said. "I don't know when you're going to get around to having it tuned. Especially in the past two years it's gone quite downhill with all the banging around it's subjected to."

The deputy judge chuckled and found his attention engaged.

"Certainly! For these calves I should have the piano tuned!" the teacher replied. "You see, I always have two or three pupils whose parents generally don't allow their children to abuse their own piano at home, when their skills are essentially non-existent, that is to say they exist just enough for them to show off with them a bit. They always excuse it by saying a bad piano must be used for teaching purposes, it would be a shame to wreck the nice piano they have at home, with the teacher's it's no matter ... That's true, with this rattletrap it really doesn't matter."

The young man looked cheerfully at the long, yellow piano which stretched itself out resignedly in the dark depths of the front room.

The lady opened up the lid, sat down behind it and, without music, lit into the keys. The young man's mouth hung open in astonishment. With stiff, outstretched fingers, as though with so many little drumsticks, she worked the keys, which began to sound in a sort of desperate confusion. Such amazing piano playing had never met his ears: it was as lively and spirited as a hussar attack and resulted in a prodigiously energetic cacaphony without so much as a single clean tone, yet was more impressive than any music he'd ever heard.

When the lady had finished, she abruptly turned around on her seat and searched the young man's face for his reaction. You see? she seemed to be saying: That's what you call piano playing! Yes, sir!

The teacher started to applaud; the deputy judge put his cigar down and joined him.

"My goodness, how you deliberated!" the lady said with a laugh.

"Not at all, I'm just so amazed! I wouldn't have dreamed I'd be hearing classical music. What was that?"

"Ah, you don't know it? The 'Song of the Birds.'"

"Marvelous! And where did you learn it?"

"Oh my, I've known that since my childhood. Received enough slaps on account of it. That's the sort of thing that must be drummed into one, like the Lord's Prayer. But rest assured, you won't be subjected to any more classical pieces."

"Ah, there's only one sort of classical music," the teacher said, "the clinking of knives and forks. It's high time I fetched us some wine."

Once again the piano stormed forth.

> One night, as I was heading for home,
> The sky broke forth in showers of light ...

the lady crooned, and the judge looked around him, uncertain whether this celestial event wasn't just then afflicting the piano itself.

Yet the scene was very sweet and cheerful. The lady sang rather in the manner of a peasant, but she looked lovely as she sat there singing before the piano, gently lifting her head, smiling as she swayed back and forth and struck the yellowed keys with her arrow-like fingers in a self-forgetful trance, as though it were the most natural thing in the world.

"By God," the deputy judge said to himself, "she's much prettier than I thought. This lighting lends her great appeal."

The appeal in the lighting lay in the fact that she sat with her back towards the window.

He was absolutely certain that something *bad* had indeed happened last night! With half-closed eyes he looked back at the teacher, utterly without sympathy, and sought the medal on his forehead.

He continued watching the young lady's fingers and saw how white, how well-proportioned and slender they were. "Such nice, small hands," he said to himself, "it would be nice to grasp them, to hold them in mine ... kiss them. But why is she so strong and self-contained. That's not very neighborly of her ..." The way she played the piano made it appear like a great exhibition of power. Her stiffly spread fingers moved strictly along the lowest joint in the middle of the hand, they lacked the grace in their movement otherwise typical of most women's hands, which fell almost petal-like over the keys.

As though seized by desire, the woman performed one song after the other. She sang and seemed to have forgotten their guest all together – she sang with warmth, with power, first impishly, then coquettishly, and then with her entire heart. The deputy judge felt quite strange. There hung in the room a foreign odor, a reminder of many previous revelries, of smoke and dust which, long since raised, had never truly settled again, of the glue of ageing furniture, the dungeonlike cool of the walls ... Now he sensed more intensely than ever before the small town soul.

"But my, how this lady plays!" he said to himself more than once, and no matter how he attended to the music, he was unable to comprehend the sameness that characterized her songs, as though the accompaniment for each were the same. He got up and stood behind the lady after the teacher had disappeared to fetch some wine.

At length he observed her fast-moving fingers and suddenly discerned their secret. The lady had deciphered the grand secret of her life's own music. She had found the true sorceress's key that enabled her to regale her company unceasingly with Hungarian folksongs. With her right hand she played the melodies, while with her left she accompanied each tone with the proper chord, as lay within her own and the instrument's capacities.

The deputy judge smiled broadly and concluded the lady was right. All of life was made simple here. It was freed of every complication, every artifice. One had only to uncover the key to life, then everything, everything became as simple as the flowing of a brook. Every pebble in its bed becomes visible ... and who would dare pretend that the brook was not beautiful! ...

He would have liked to solve the mystery of this woman through some miracle, some random stroke of luck, as the only way it would uncover itself to him was of its own volition.

With half-closed eyes he thought of what treasures go to waste in unworthy hands. Unworthy is he who possesses them, who holds them, as is the fate in which they wither and evaporate, without redemption ...

Doltish nobodies come and, with primitive fingers, drum out the eternal melody lying dormant within the soul of this woman, much as she does that lying within the piano, and sounds are produced ... He who can discern just how he must strike an instrument will coax sounds from it ... No matter how or like what. Since helter-skelter tones are also tones, the vibration of a single chord is itself music of a sort ... No artist will ever succeed in playing the symphony of love residing in the souls of such ladies.

Individual tones. One here, one there. How pleasant if a chord happens to come together from them. Only noisy chaos clatters along through life, and she herself, as her nerves slowly decay, does not even suspect how she resembles the aged piano that is wrecked by so many clumsy pupils' hands – and which is in such great need of tuning.

Wistfully and with a twinge of pain he sensed how dearly he himself would like to take on this tuning work. But was he the right man for the job? Who had what it took to work on the instrument of a woman's soul? Everyone seeks to play on such an instrument, yet even the greatest virtuoso is a clueless dilettante in this area who has not even progressed as far in his art as has this woman in her piano playing.

He was overcome by tender affection. He would have loved to lean over the chair and rest his face on the lady's soft brown hair as it lay across her beautifully formed head like a generous pillow. He felt so trusting, so naïve, as though he were a student who stood before his ideal love and felt as happy as one who has returned home from foreign lands. To his love? To his wife? To his partner! ...

He could have cried in his joy. A cheap oriental rug lay spread across the floor, he would have loved to sit down on it and rest his head on the woman's lap and daydream or slumber there as if he were resting on the softly-clothed lap of his mother, his beloved, his wife. His heart pounded and shuddered, a dreamy sense of bliss flooded his soul, he had no logical explanation for his condition, and he said to himself: *Romance will never pass from mankind.*

"Sing a song from the olden days ..." he said during a brief pause.

Without hesitation or reflection, the lady sang:

Wither, wither, fade away,
Why does your cheery bloom persist?
The burning sun has made its mark,
Wither, violet mine.

Carefully I've tended you
Beside my little window,
Watering you day and night,
Feeding your brown earth ...

The sweet sounds filled the room, and the piano, whose G key hadn't sounded for a quarter hour yet suddenly awakened to new life, harmonized wondrously with the tones ...

Tears welled in the deputy judge's eyes, and he stretched out his arms and wrapped them around the lady's beautiful white neck where it rose from the neckline of her blue polka-dot blouse.

"Magnificent ..."

The lady, though overcome by a similar mood, stood up abruptly and flashed a scornful look.

Even before she'd pushed them away, his arms withdrew, and the lady's disdainful gaze met the man's sober, self-deprecating regard.

The woman didn't say a word. She stood and left the room. The man took his cigar from the table. He saw with pleasure that it hadn't gone out, it still emitted a thin stream of smoke.

"Of course," he said to himself, "music is possessed of a simple key! One starts at the beginning and continues on until the end ... One never begins at the end!"

He plopped himself down in the armchair and stared vacantly.

He had to get up. He didn't feel well. His mood grew pained and something pricked him. A spring was poking through the threadbare upholstery.

He was seized by a sense of unease. His blood eddied and swirled within him and he began pacing back and forth in the room with deliberate steps, as though he were walking about the deck of a ship.

He felt like he'd sunk into a deep and noxious stratum of life of which he had until now been completely unaware and where myriad dangers loomed overhead.

At that point he smiled and said to himself cynically, that it was all so much asininity. His excitement was mere artifice. The problem was that he'd never before had dealings with a respectable woman of the so-called petite bourgeoisie. And yet it was all so simple. An old, feckless husband and a fiery, hedonistic wife ... For he who must, it suffices to reach out his hand and pluck ... She won't give herself to everyone with equal ease ... Sadly, he was a bit *distingué* for this woman, who until then had only had experience with schoolteachers and, at best, curates. And now she was holding back somewhat, the beast.

The *beast*! The word pleased him. He clung to it and repeated it to himself. From it he derived strength and courage. After all, it was only natural that this beast had relations with everyone, that she was cuckolding her husband! ...

The door opened and the teacher entered. He carried several bottles of wine. In each hand he bore two or three bottles, which he held awkwardly by the necks between his fingers.

"Well," he said with satisfaction, "we've nothing to fear now, judge sir! ..."

He set the bottles down in the cool corner of the room and chatted cheerfully. "The cellar is a ways away. But at least it's a fine cellar. A dry one. Better than that of the cooperative. And I sent my nephew to get the curate."

The judge was thunderstruck. He gaped at the teacher, as though it were impossible to understand such a simple utterance. He could not perceive the slightest mystery behind the little man's thick moustache. Veres acted entirely as though everything were in perfect order; he had a dear guest before him whom he wished to entertain, and as he sought to augment the company, he sent his nephew after the curate.

"I'm glad," the deputy judge responded with an exaggerated air of importance, "after all, it's important that I see all the players assembled together ... Just put your trust in me, then everything will come out all right."

The teacher didn't answer, he merely smiled faintly. "So where is my wife?" he asked. "The poor thing is no doubt up to her ears with the cooking. I definitely took her by surprise today. But that does a woman no harm. It only becomes clear what sort of a housewife one is when unexpected guests come to visit."

The day maid entered the room, a skinny Slovak woman with her hair tied in a scarf, and began setting the table.

The two men stood at the window, having downed a glass or two of wine, and sought to distract themselves as they waited for the meal to start.

The deputy judge was curious what sort of look the wife would have on her face when she entered.

She came in red-faced, one could see she'd been working in the kitchen, but nothing beyond that.

Where do these people keep their souls, the young man thought to himself, and looked at the one spouse and then the other. The teacher offered his guest a place at the table as though there were no more natural thing in the world than that he should dine with them today, while his wife echoed the invitation in the kind of straightforward manner that made it seem like they were all the oldest of friends and he'd had this dinner date on his calendar for months.

"How do you like it here in our little town?" the lady asked him.

"I like it very much."

"Naturally there are many lovely women here … Are you courting a great number of them?"

"I wouldn't know where to start."

"Well! … Among the upper ten thousand they're fairly crawling with beauties."

The deputy judge flashed a forced smile. "Where are these upper ten thousand, then?" he asked.

"Somewhere up among the stars," the lady said with a mordant smile. "Where there are nothing but officers and officers' wives, attorneys' wives, the notary's wife, the circuit judge's wife with her six starlets, her six girls, and you young men can breathe in the celestial air there! …"

Bitter sarcasm hung in her voice, and the deputy judge sensed how touchy an issue this was for her and that it wouldn't behoove him to utter a response.

"Ha, there one can afford *anything*!" the lady spoke. "Where there is extravagance, there is money. The notary rakes in at least fifteen thousand, so his wife can go around in the latest fashions like a lady from Budapest."

The deputy judge had finished his soup, which had been oversalted and tasted as though it had sat out for too long, and he sat picturing to himself the notary's wife. He'd always regarded her as a very distinguished, tasteful gentlewoman. When he compared her apartment with the one in which he now found himself, he was struck by the disparity between the two. There everything was subdued, harmonious, artistic, while here garish, cheap color prints hung on the wall, two little images, the one depicting a happy young couple, the other a sulky one ... On the opposite wall ... a piece featuring a crown within a frame.

The lady laughed loudly, painfully, gratingly.

"Or the mayor's girls! Their noses are so snubby that the rain falls directly inside them, yet they still manage to stick them in the air! But when they don their red dresses, they are indeed splendid! Like flies in red raspberry juice."

The young man laughed and, his eyebrows raised, recalled the homely, yet appealing gypsy girls; they were extraordinarily attractive in their red dresses ... played tennis very cleverly ...

"Certainly it will be a stab in your heart when I cast *aspersions* on your idols."

"Nothing of the sort, I have no idols ..."

"But it couldn't possibly please you for me to mention the doctor's wife, little Aranka."

The young man blushed ever so slightly. "Please, feel free."

"There's no need to blush! I congratulate you on your good taste! Tisk, tisk! If, God forbid, the wind were to blow on her, it would blow her away, all the way to Bratislava and beyond!"

The deputy judge laughed out loud. "Why Bratislava?"

The lady laughed without answering. "Please, have some meat ... Not that bony piece, take this one ... You really need to get married, you don't even know how to select a savory morsel from the serving dish. I've no idea who you'll end up marrying, though, when you choose like that."

"Well," the teacher chimed in, "marriage is a good deal like baked chicken."

The deputy judge had heard this comparison at least a hundred times, but the more he heard it, the less he understood why the saying was so popular.

"A man never knows what he's actually choosing. I seek out the thigh meat, and I get the breast instead!" the teacher pursued his joke.

The lady paid no attention to his words. "Have you made your choice?" she asked the young man.

"Me?"

"Certainly not I!"

The young man's blood shot to his brain. He cast a sidelong glance at the teacher, who was frightfully busy nibbling the tendons and cartilage from the bony piece the lady had kept him from taking, then he looked audaciously into her eyes, injecting his complete devotion into his gaze, and said: "I've already made my selection."

"Who, then?"

"Who? ..."

"Is she blonde?"

The young man held his gaze and shook his head.

"Brunette?"

"Neither blonde nor brunette."

"In true Hungarian manner!" the teacher spoke, and he looked up triumphantly, having succeeded in mastering the chicken bone with his bad teeth. He laid the bone with much decorum onto the edge of his plate and wiped his greasy hands vigorously with the oversized napkin. "I too chose one like that!" he added.

The lady and the young man smiled at each other. Then they laughed: they'd understood one another.

"Well, isn't it so?" the teacher continued. "Is my wife blonde? or brunette? Do you know what I fell in love with when I saw her for the very first time? ... Her gold tooth! ...By God! Had it not been for this gold tooth, I would never have noticed her! After all, she has no other striking feature."

"You old donkey!" the lady laughed, and her gold tooth twinkled, but sensing that the judge was looking at it, she hid it with her napkin.

"Absolutely! I'd barely laid eyes on her when her gold tooth sparkled at me! By George, I said to myself, *that* makes her a pretty girl!"

"Shut your mouth," the little lady said, laughing out loud.

Then they clinked glasses.

"Whether you believe it or not ..." the deputy judge said to the lady, "yesterday evening when they told me that you were the teacher's wife, I asked myself if you weren't the beautiful little lady who had a golden tooth!?"

"It's clear you can't hold your wine!"

They laughed.

"Certainly, my dear," the teacher spoke, "this tooth of yours has truly paid off. Without it you would never have gotten married!"

"Unfortunate enough that it happened. But if it gets me a nice suitor, then I'll forgive it for the fact that I had it put in."

The door opened and the curate entered along with the student. "Good day to you!" the curate greeted them. "You're only just eating now?"

"Come over here!" the teacher said, rising from his seat. He approached the curate and shook his hand, then tried to introduce the two strangers to each other, but he still did not know the deputy judge's name; he overcame the hurdle by saying: "Meet the curate, deputy judge sir!"

The two young men shook hands, and each mumbled something between his teeth, doubtless his own name.

"Come then, have a seat," the lady said, casually extending her hand to the curate.

"I've already had dinner ..."

"No matter, just have a seat. You too, Laci ... You must be quite hungry, aren't you, Laci?"

Her voice was tender, almost pleading, apologetic even. The youth failed to respond, he sat down at the foot of the table and remained there with eyes lowered. The judge stared intently at him. The youth appeared sullen, but nothing suggested that he faced a significant turn of fate, nor that anything had brought about any unusual emotion in him. He ate hungrily, almost ravenously, and apart from his spoon nothing seemed to interest him.

The curate struck the deputy judge as a quiet, happy little man, like someone who is not accustomed to troubling the waters and exerts his presence in a way that attracts no one's attention.

What could the lady have wanted with these two children!

"So what have you been doing today?" the wife asked the curate. The deputy judge's heart beat heavily; he observed with bitterness that the *túrós csusza* the maid brought in, that traditional quark cheese noodle dish he so loved, was not prepared with dumplings as was customary in the Hungarian plains region, but with long, thin noodles. He was more than tired of the fact that in this town every dish was prepared differently from in his homeland. It was as though he had to relearn how to eat from the ground up, as if he were living abroad ... How many Hungaries were there in this country! How many types of cuisine! ...

"I was asleep," the curate said, smiling. "I slept like a log."

He stared at the woman with a rather tired expression, as though forgetting his eyes over her. They were firmly attached to her. Then he yawned lustily.

"You're quite the great hero!" the lady laughed.

The buttery smell of the *túrós csusza* rose up the deputy judge's nose! He was just holding the dish in his hand and was about to serve himself, but suddenly he put it down. A feeling of bitterness overcame him. He felt himself a stranger who didn't belong here. Why was he here, what did he want, what was he after! Why had he ever set foot in this place, in this entire town? He'd come in order to stab his own self in the heart! What an impossible position he'd gotten himself into! Wasn't it horrible enough that he was on the same social level with callow youths ... Now he was to compete with this nobody for the lady's heart ... Ridiculous! What does he want with her heart. She has no heart! Her body – that's what has him so excited! And he won't let up now – not until he possesses her!

"Don't you enjoy dishes prepared with butter?" the lady asked, and the deputy judge felt her voice caress and fondle him like a spring breeze.

He smiled and looked into her eyes. The lady's regard was spiteful, yet he was convinced that her gaze was directed solely at him! That she could only look that way at him! ... If a suitable opportunity presented itself, she wouldn't hesitate a single moment to devote her body entirely to him.

His face burned, his blood boiled, and he sensed his own virility, and failed to understand how it came that this woman's proximity filled him with such sensual impulses.

"There's no need to undergo any torture today, we also have dumplings without butter ... I thought you didn't like ..."

She struck her glass with her knife and soon the Slovak woman brought in the dumplings, prepared in the manner of the plains region, with cheese curds and cream.

"What a cunning woman! If she had to cater to the wishes of a hundred men, she would discern the taste of each and every one!" the teacher spoke.

The deputy judge's expression darkened somewhat. What if the man were right ...

But as he ate his *túrós csusza* with gusto, with an almost sensual greed, he calmed down. He could not own this woman. She had a husband – doubtless she had others' husbands as well ... No matter, as long as he got his own share. And if his instincts were right, he most certainly would! He would get precisely the share of her that he needed ...

There was a knock at the door.

"Come in!" the teacher and his wife called out simultaneously.

The parson entered, followed by Dvihally.

The old parson was a heavy-set Lutheran pastor with a broad face. His visage was pained yet satisfied, like that of people who have no troubles in their souls, only with their gout and their asthma.

The teacher sprang up and greeted him loudly: "Welcome, honored sir! Please come inside!" And: "Good afternoon, my friend," he added, turning to his colleague.

The parson shook the teacher's hand; in that very moment, his eyes found those of the teacher's wife. The deputy judge, who stood along with the curate and the student in honor of the guests, grasped the parson's look and shuddered. Was the entire world in love with this woman?

As he shook the old parson's hand, he assessed him with a hostile look. So that was the pastor whom the fat butcher had chosen for the short period of time until his son would be eligible for election. The old sinner – and during this short time he would lust after this woman. The old man's supplicating gaze gave him a bit of hope. It seemed to signify that something had already happened between them. Perhaps he had already attempted to approach her and the lady had sent him on his way! ... He now turned his attention to black-haired Dvihally, who in this moment was holding the lady's hand. Immediately he saw, he knew, that he too was enamored of her! ... For what a long time he held her hand! ... And how the frosty-tempered man melted, who was normally so stiff and brittle that every frozen feature of his face creaked.

What a nice group of people has gathered together here, he said to himself.

He turned toward the window and his eyes burned. He thought of leaving this place immediately. He wasn't the fool to let pointless yearning consume him! For such a worthless creature! ... He'd already been made foolish enough – the devil take the whole affair! What did he have in common with this woman? She was neither pretty, nor intelligent, nor kind! For her he should be made a fool of? He could still go, as of yet it wasn't too late. His heart wouldn't break from grief!

In this moment the lady passed him from the back and brushed against his face with her soft, naked elbow.

He closed his eyes and let his blood hurtle effervescently through his veins.

Moments passed and he didn't dare to open his eyelids, as he felt that would cause the voluptuous sensation to end. On his face the spot where the lady's skin had contacted his own burned; his blood had gone mad, and as it coursed from one end of his body to the other, it rushed again and again back to that spot, like some wild pack that sensed across the stone wall that there beyond lay its prey, ready to give itself up, yet impossible to pounce on.

The group grew silent, as though their conversation had been cut off. The one trimmed his cigar onto the edge of his plate, the other adjusted his shirt cuffs or coughed, but for a time they all lost their heads. The parson was pale, the curate blushed, the student shivered, the teacher's eyes stared wide open, while Dvihally's eyelids sunk to his pupils and he stared as motionlessly before him as a fakir.

Everyone had noticed that touch.

And as, after a brief and painful pause, each looked at the other, it was suddenly clear to everyone what was transpiring. They all looked at one another as if the scales had fallen from their eyes, and the moment the one's glance met the other's he immediately looked nervously and perplexedly away.

Six men and one woman. And all six were seized with the same consuming passion for that one woman. All six bore the same loathing for the others and each was ready to engage in a self-sacrificing fight to the end with the others.

The silence had already lasted too long. The deputy judge gathered his courage and glanced quickly at the others in the room. He saw impassive and expressionless faces and was relieved that, in his mind, no one had noticed anything.

The lady stood at the sideboard with her back turned toward the company. She busied herself noisily with the fruit plates, and as she turned around, she saw with pleasure that the deputy judge was as lively and relaxed as he should be. It wasn't entirely clear to her own self what she'd just done. In reality, it was nothing. She sensed that this one man wanted to leave from here, and with her womanly instinct it was this one man that she wished to keep here.

Thank God, she said to herself, *that no one noticed it. Otherwise what must they think!*

She smiled, as she didn't regard what she'd done as anything significant.

The student rotated and twirled his glass in his hand. He stared distractedly before him.

"What will become of that glass!" his uncle yelled at him. His voice sounded unusually powerful, it thundered coarsely as it broke the silence. "Useless pest! Staring at nothing with your stupid calves' eyes ... I'll teach you to wander around at night!"

He banged his knife clangorously against his plate. The lady listened to him in wonder.

"If you please, Reverend," the teacher turned to the old parson, "this is the kind of ne'er-do-well a man raises for himself. This sort of loafer, this gadabout ... Last night we were sitting to dine at this very table, he of course with us! So I tell him, 'go and attend to your studies!' What does he do? He gets up, leaves, and returns home in the morning. They're going to throw him out of school."

The lady's blood froze in her veins. She looked in shock at her husband's face. Not once did he return her gaze, and yet she knew his words were aimed at her.

"And rightly so. A vagabond like him doesn't belong among educated people. Where were you roaming about, huh?"

The youth furrowed his brow and answered, his voice cracking, yet strong: "I didn't go anywhere. I sat in my room and studied."

"Keep jabbering on like that, and I'll let you have it. We're not in the headmaster's office. You can lie to his face, claim you didn't run into him during the night. But I'll beat you so hard you still feel it when ..."

"What is the matter, please?" the parson asked, and the furrows in his face revealed his sympathetic bewilderment.

"The entire town saw him gadding about at night in places that are never frequented by decent people."

"I wasn't anywhere!" the youth cried tearfully, "I was sitting here in my room studying, and then ... I mean, wasn't it I who took the curate into his room?!"

The curate stared at him in horror, his mouth agape. In silent, wordless wonder he nodded, as though attempting to force his memory to recollect what possibly could have happened.

"Of course," the lady said.

"Nonsense!" the husband said with a shrug of his shoulders, but he would not have looked at his wife for anything in the world. "The headmaster told me that he himself saw him on the street."

"So?"

"What do you mean, 'so'?"

"What did Laci say to that?"

"What! He lied that it wasn't true. As though the headmaster would lie ... And the scoundrel cut the buttons off of his own jacket."

The lady looked intently at the young man and smiled to see that two buttons were missing from his jacket. And, sweet boy, not from the jacket he'd worn the day before.

"What sort of talk is this!" she cried. "So I'm lying, Laci's lying, and the headmaster too? So what is the truth then? Ridiculous."

"It's not ridiculous, it's terribly sad. That the youth of today is so shameless ... Loitering about the entire night long in hovels! ..."

"What do you mean, the entire night long!" the lady bristled, and her large, dark eyes all but shot forth sparks. "He was here at midnight! No? Perhaps he was out before midnight, perhaps he left again after midnight ... In truth, when I went into his room this morning, his face did look as though he hadn't slept ... Have I guessed right, Laci?"

The youth, who listened to the lady's words in amazement, lowered his head and cowered in shame and guilt.

"Always making something out of nothing! That's what you men are good at! Rather than finding out what's actually true." She laughed and her gold tooth sparkled from between her full, red, beautifully formed lips.

The deputy judge released a laugh. "Well, Mr. Bovary, there we have the truth," he said as he reached for his glass.

They clinked glasses. The student did not lift his glass, he merely peered for a moment with head lowered at the men as they drank.

But everyone fell silent and drank their wine without speaking.

"We'll see what the truth is when they throw the young gentleman out of school," the teacher said moodily as he dried his great, wine-dampened moustache with his napkin.

The student rose, nodded his head at the company, and sought to excuse himself.

"Such a worthless fellow," his uncle exclaimed. "Bringing shame on me at this point in time … You! Did you encounter the headmaster or not?"

"Of course he encountered him," the lady answered, helping the young man out.

But the youth lowered his head in sullen silence.

"Get out of my sight, before I tear you to pieces," the little teacher growled, then turned away from him.

The student exited out the door, his head drawn down between his shoulders. As he closed the door behind him, the men exchanged animated looks. One rival had left and abundant fodder for discussion remained behind.

"What was that?" the parson asked sanctimoniously.

Everyone had a response, and ultimately the teacher, who waxed unusually loquacious, recounted the entire story from beginning to end, with the unwavering attention to detail that a small-town inhabitant employs when telling the same story for the tenth time.

The deputy judge listened distractedly. He looked at the tall, iron stove that had been polished clean with "silver powder," its door alone revealing traces of black smoke around the edges, along with its pipes, stained in places by soot. The pipes were in fact rather beat up. Then he looked out through the window at the church. The church stood in the courtyard, surrounded by houses and tall picket fences, with only its façade visible from the street. It was an old Catholic edifice, with Gothic windows and tall, plain pillars, but it was the Lutherans who'd erected the tower upon it, which was built in a commonplace Romanesque style, its only interesting feature being that a dwelling for the tower watchman was located beneath the bells with a gallery surrounding it, but it was so low that anyone expecting it to provide a decent view would be quite disappointed. The horn of the tower guard jutted out displeasingly from the corner. The chancel with its low roof hid like a frightened lamb behind the tall nave. The walls were weathered, the lilac red plaster was falling off in large chunks, allowing the gray mortar and dark-colored brick framework to show through. The church, this house of God, was as sad as an orphan without a caregiver, just like this town, this people, this life that unfolded around it. A peasant girl walked below along the other side of the street, her dark-brown dress embroidered with pale red flowers. Her grass-green apron string was visible from a distance and her dirty, blackened feet bounced with each step. For a moment, as she passed across the window, the deputy judge's face lit up; these peasants still retained a remnant of nature's beauty. A peasant man now crossed in front of the window. A wondrous sight. He'd placed his narrow-brimmed cap over his head like some regal crown; the shaggy cloak hung in such a lordly manner from his shoulders that it resembled a pelisse adorned with precious stones, and he bore himself so sturdily and strode along with such self-confidence in his simple drawstring shoes, as though the proud glory of ancient lords had left its noble traces behind in him. And yet what a sad little man he was, illiterate, innumerate, unacquainted with luxury, and what unbelievably filthy rags he clothed himself in to elevate his humanity ...

"They certainly won't expel him!" the curate spoke up and, forgetting himself, looked reassuringly at the lady.

The gentlemen were all indignant over the young man's audacity, but the moment they discovered the flash of joy that lit up the lady's face, they immediately came to their senses.

"It would be ludicrous to expel someone over such a petty affair …"

"Of course it's ludicrous!" his superior, the old parson said sternly, his lips quivering, "but nonetheless it can still happen."

"Well if it happens, then I will leave this town at once," the lady stated with grim determination.

The men blinked in wonder. They drank without cease and this made it seem to them all the more impossible that the lady should leave Ilosva. And the deputy judge perceived their situation with utter clarity: these people were bound to the land! Never, ever would they be able to leave this town, were they to live for a hundred years, even were a catastrophe to turn the earth upside down … Only here at home were they people, men, somebodies. If they were to leave this place, every accomplishment of their lives heretofore would immediately evaporate … And he suddenly realized how they, too, were all drawn to this woman. She was an outsider, from another town, a different people, she'd arrived here a stranger and had certainly remained one; and marriage was to her a matter of duty. Of course she wasn't at home, not among relatives, not with her people: she did not bear the full weight of the local atmosphere. Once again it was the Trojan War, the battle for a woman. And in the background, Greek history: the battle between villages.

"Even the most unheard of things can happen!" the parson stated anew. "I can imagine that, if this young man stood by himself, his career would be threatened by the most egregious catastrophe. But naturally, a person does not come from a good family and have neighbors, friends, and family connections so that, because of a rare misstep, his life should be ruined ... Have no fear, dear lady, I will manage this entire affair at the next meeting of the supervisory council."

The lady regarded the old parson's goodhearted countenance warmly, gratefully, and reached out her hand to him. "I thank you, dear Reverend."

The aged cleric held her hand at length, patting it with eagerness.

Dvihally blinked dismally. "It's rather late for that," he said, daring to disparage the parson's proposal. "What can be done once the matter comes before the supervisory council! Something has to happen before these idiots make of this an earth-shattering affair. Tomorrow afternoon there'll be a meeting at the savings bank. I'll say my piece to the headmaster. He's in our hands! I'll wring his neck if he so much as tries to flinch."

"There's no point in any of that!" the curate jumped in. "It's do or die! I'll go after him today yet; if he doesn't call off his plan, I'll box his ears and challenge him to a duel."

"Oh, how sweet of you," the lady said with a laugh, and patted the young man's reddened face.

"Honored sir," the old parson countered him, "have you lost your senses? To say such a thing! The idea of it! For this one utterance you could forfeit your entire priestly career. I alone have the means to help this poor boy!"

"No, only I do!" Dvihally cried.

Silence reigned for a moment. The lady took great pleasure in this competition, the deputy judge found it amusing.

"I alone have the means!" the husband now asserted in a decisive tone.

Everyone fell silent at this. Dvihally lit up a new cigar, the curate poured more wine. They drank.

"How so?" all three of them asked at once.

The teacher hesitated. "I don't know yet," he said moodily, "but I'll find a way."

For several minutes, the silence weighed down on them. Everyone interpreted the teacher's words as evidence of his desire, on the basis of his rights and duties as husband, to steal the others' thunder. They felt like they had gone farther than common human empathy allowed. They knew that Pál Veres was a very patient husband, doubtless with good reason. But nonetheless only he was the husband, and if he wanted he could scatter the entire company to the four winds.

To their joy, the door opened and a guest entered.

A slender lady with a sickly face stepped inside.

"Welcome, dear Toncsi!" the woman of the house greeted her, rushing over to her with exaggerated enthusiasm.

"Ah, Mrs. Dvihally!" the man of the house spoke, and in that instant his face softened and he fled, he raced with glee away from the moment when he had had to torment himself with burdensome feelings. Such a life was no life. It gave one a headache and ruined one's good humor. The only way to live was frivolously. Flitting and leaping playfully and flying from every real worry and concern. In this way alone was life possible to bear, but spending more than a single minute troubling oneself over some difficult matter – that was too unpleasant! The teacher's face glowed as he greeted his friend's wife, as though true happiness had been accorded him.

All the gentlemen stood and took the guest's hand. They, too, sensed relief, as though they'd been liberated from a demon. This feeling of liberation poured forth from the man of the house, nonetheless Veres's relaxed cheerfulness struck them as almost excessive. As his smiling regard passed from the guest one by one to the others, they could not help but look for a latent expression of hatred. They found no trace of it. The man of the house had become a true *major domo* who, having shaken off the unpleasantness of domestic squabbling and worries, transformed instantly, the moment someone opened the door, into that one truly happy man in the world whose shirt the fairytale king seeks.

"Welcome to our home! How nice of you to stop by for a visit. Brava, dear friend! One must truly get out of the house from time to time, but let us now drink to the health of our friend! By George!"

The deputy judge grasped the guest's slender, wrinkled, washed out hand, and quietly mumbled his name to her.

"Do you not know the judge?" the lady of the house asked. "Our deputy judge here was very kind today, my husband dragged him to our home and he made no resistance. And he's all but dying of boredom."

"On the contrary, I feel quite comfortable here!"

"A toast, a toast! Egad! The deputy judge hasn't once emptied his glass. That's not how it's done! You've got to drain your glass! Drink up, for cripes sake!"

They laughed. Whoever could see them in that moment would not have dreamt that quarrels and petulance, jealous anger and murderous hatred had ever existed between them. A mirthful and relaxed company was assembled here who, unaffected by malice, coexisted in cheerful harmony.

"Oh, I certainly don't drink!" the guest spoke. "Absolutely not, but thank you."

"She doesn't drink," Dvihally confirmed, tipping his glass toward his wife. "Even if the doctor prescribes it, one can't get a single drop down her."

"Well, then let's drink up her portion for her!" the man of the house cried. "By George! It's her loss! And our gain!"

They clinked their glasses together, and the two ladies went through the open door into the drawing room.

"How are you, dear Toncsi?" asked the lady of the house, then pushed a book or two on the round table off to the side.

"Well enough, I suppose," the guest sighed in a tone that suggested she hadn't the smallest bit of lung in her body and with the sort of grief she would express if a funeral were taking place in her home.

"And your maid, Agnes, has she already made some improvement?"

"Ah, nothing good will ever come of her! I get so angry that sometimes I think the devil has gotten hold of me. Imagine what she did recently. I have an alarm clock, already quite old, which won't run unless one stands it on its head. So recently I went out into the kitchen, she having just wiped off the dishes, and the wretch, instead of putting them away, takes the clock in hand and removes the screws, then starts tinkering with it. What are you doing there! I tell her when I open the door to see what's going on, because it's so quiet in that kitchen. As you can imagine, I practically had a stroke when I saw that she was tinkering with the clock. What are you doing there! Well, she just starts bursting out laughing, and says she's going to fix it!"

She fell silent, as she sensed bitter gall rising in her throat.

The lady of the house laughed and raged at once. "Scandalous! What wretches! And then?"

"So then I grabbed it from her and I look at it, turn it this way and that, and it doesn't work! Now she's ruined that, too! Imagine, now that clock won't run – only if it's turned onto its left side."

"Servants certainly cause a lot of bother."

"I've never had this much bother with any of them! She's a veritable demon. Since the moment she set foot in our home, nothing is in its proper place – I look for the dust cloth, it's nowhere to be found, I look for the dish towel, it's gone. Where is it? Nowhere! I end up using the bottom of my skirt to dust with! Did you know, dust lies everywhere in thick layers. I tell her there will be bean soup for dinner, so she has to peel potatoes. We usually put those in."

"I do as well, we like it better that way."

"So, I tell her to peel potatoes to put into the bean soup. Fine. Later it occurs to me that I can't eat beans, as the baby cries immediately. This nursing business is so bothersome, you're absolutely right not to have any children. A woman as old as I, and here I am still nursing children! ..."

She fell silent for a moment, heaved a sigh, then continued: "Yes, right, so I tell her, peel the potatoes, Agnes. But then I remember I can't eat any beans, so at least we can prepare a little goulash, I'll eat a bit of that. So I tell her, Agnes, we'll have goulash. We won't use the beans in the soup, do you understand? I tell her, they'll be a side dish. Once more I ask her, do you understand? Of course, she understands everything! – but she pays attention to nothing. So do you know what that wretch did? She put the potatoes into the bean dish."

"What impudence!"

"Even though she knew full well that, when we cook the beans as a side dish, we never put potatoes in with them."

"No, I don't add potatoes to my bean dishes either!"

"So I give her the diapers to wash. Imagine, when I go to the linen chest to find them, I pull them out filthy dirty. I nearly had a stroke. I've never encountered such incompetence! And she just howls with laughter, squealing and whinnying, whenever she does something stupid, until she's practically rolling on the floor. As if it would ever occur to her to lay a carpet out straight! Oh, the edges on those! Every corner is wrinkled and frayed! She's already ruined my carpets to the point where they'll never lie flat again. Nothing is spared from her havoc, she's careless with everything, purposefully ruining everything she touches – my life is already such a living hell that I left our place to come here just so I could catch my breath for a bit."

"Well, why don't you get rid of her?"

"What can I do?" she moaned like someone sick with fever who laments that it's not possible to rid oneself of the illness, it must be endured until it turns for the good or the bad of its own accord. "What can I do when I've no one else. Where can I find another one when each is worse than the other. And I have to pay her eight forints, and today she tells me she's going to Pest as a parlormaid!"

The lady of the house laughed out loud. "As a parlormaid! That's just the thing for her."

"But picture it," the guest sobbed on, "she told me that in Pest she'd get twelve forints right off the bat."

"You don't say!"

"And that Matykó's girl also earns that."

"That's a lot of loot."

"They're all the same these days. You're lucky that it's just you alone, but I with my five children ... And to be nursing on top of that! ... These men are so insensitive. They have no regard for a poor woman. If only the devil would take me away from here, so I wouldn't have to trouble myself with this wretch any longer. And she's greedy too, this afternoon again as I was leaving I caught

173

her standing over the saucepan with a spoon, skimming the fat from the boiled milk and gorging herself with it, then acting as though nothing had happened. Lightning should strike such people. Nothing remains of the food she takes from the dinner table. In fact yesterday we'd barely only tasted the salad dish, I go out and find her eating, her plate piled high, and I mean high, and she's shoveling it in, the sauce dripping from both sides of her mouth, she's stuffing her face to the point where she can barely swallow, and she grabs a huge chunk of bread and shoves it down her throat. Hey, you, I say to her, can't you at least eat with a bit more refinement? Yes, I can, she says, then starts cackling until she nearly bursts. That's my fate, that people like that should mock me."

The lady of the house listened with rapt attention. "Oh my. I'm certainly fortunate with regard to our maid, it's as though she weren't even here. That's the best way to have things; she just does her work and leaves. I'm happy when I never see her."

"You're lucky in everything. But if you had five children, she wouldn't stay with you. And she wouldn't be enough. When I only had one or two children, I had no thought of hiring a maid, I barely knew what a maid was. Let the devil suffer with them. But now!"

The deputy judge entered the drawing room. "Are you ladies trafficking in secrets?"

"Naturally, and with big ones!" the lady of the house remarked with a laugh. "Ones that concern you. Too bad you didn't hear them."

"It's truly a fine thing," the deputy judge said as he sat down in the armchair the lady pushed over toward him, "when women are discussing household matters. First the servants take a turn, then the men, after that of course dresses, female friends, and then gossip."

"How do you know that so well?"

"I too was once a young boy, and in those days I always hung onto my mother's skirt."

"That's how you became such a big skirt-chaser!"

The deputy judge laughed. "Is that what you think?"

"I heard it! And that you're quite promiscuous. And rather than chase after the girls, you're always running after the ladies."

"The ladies?"

"To no avail, it's not the pretty one who's pretty, right, Toncsi?"

"Rather the one whom a person likes!" Toncsi said.

"The pretty one is the one a person likes."

"The one you like strikes you as pretty."

"Fine, then. You're beautiful and I like you. Now I'd like to know whether you're pretty because I like you, or do I like you because you're pretty."

The lady of the house laughed out loud at every word. But the appearance of the curate in the door left her with no chance to respond.

"Pardon me," he said, poking his head inside the doorway, "there is such an interesting conversation unfolding here that I, too, would be so bold ..."

"You just wait outside there. You don't understand the language being spoken here. That's just what we need, to ruin the saintly little theology student."

Incapable of making even the smallest witticism, the curate simply smiled.

"The saints are often more corrupt than the demons," the deputy judge quipped.

"You're certainly right there!" the lady of the house responded, laughing at the curate with a warm, radiant gaze.

The deputy judge's expression grew more serious. But it was little more than a brief twitching of his face. Only Mrs. Dvihally had noticed it, who was eyeing his face with acute attention.

"Have a seat!" the lady of the house spoke to the curate; immediately he followed her order and sat down.

Did something really happen last night? the deputy judge asked himself.

The lady's brown eyes twinkled at him and in that moment he forgot everything.

"You have a very charming home," he said absent-mindedly.

"Do I?" the lady laughed, then curled her lips in disgust. "It's a shabby, dilapidated abode."

The deputy judge smiled and looked around the vaulted room. He understood her. Seen from afar, such a nook is pretty and quaint, but an aspiring woman has different desires nowadays. A bright, shiny, clean dwelling with mirror-windows and a balcony. And perhaps rightly so.

"Soon we'll have a nice home," Mrs. Dvihally said, "in the new building."

"Of course," the lady of the house responded scornfully, "only you'll have some waiting to do. Unless you think the mayor will put up with the schoolteachers having a nicer home than he has. He's settled himself down in his own shabby, mold-infested house, so he won't let anyone have a nicer home than him. Think of the grammar school building. There they ruined the headmaster's quarters so thoroughly that one can barely live there. And all because the mayor begrudged a teacher having a respectable home."

"How do you know the headmaster's home?" the deputy judge asked.

"I know it, what's that to you?"

"Pardon me!"

The lady released a good-humored laugh and added by way of appeasing him: "One shouldn't seek to know everything, it just ages a person."

But while she said that, she became distracted, and thought to herself how she should go herself to visit the headmaster. Then maybe nothing would happen to her little nephew.

"So that's how things work?" the deputy judge asked. "To engage in such aggressive tactics over petty, small-minded jealousy."

"And not for the first time!" the lady said with a guffaw. "Do you know how the town wrestled with getting the military here? No? Well, it happened as follows, at some point the emperor himself ordered that Ilosva should have a military presence, since Ilosva was naturally such a magnificent town that it was impossible to imagine it without a military. All well and good, but then the town decided that, thanks but no thanks, we'd rather not. Then later, when the town did in fact want to have the army here, the higher-ups said that no soldiers were available! Whew, what running around it cost to arrive at an understanding with the duke that they should send a garrison here. In fact, in the end it was only a home-defense corps."

"So why did the town refuse a garrison at first?"

"Because at that time the mayor's wife was still young. He was afraid of the officers."

Raucous laughter ensued.

"And do you know why the military is needed now?"

"Why?"

"Because the mayor's daughters are ready to be married off. Maybe some little officers can have their happiness ruined by them!"

The old parson appeared in the doorway.

"Oh, oh," he said with pastoral gentleness, "how nicely you're amusing yourselves! And you let us sit out there boring ourselves."

"Come sit here beside me, holy father!" the lady of the house said playfully.

In no way did the parson acknowledge the impudence in the lady's words, on the contrary, he endeavored to reciprocate her childlike spirit and planted himself impishly on an armchair.

"Time to rejuvenate myself," he said.

"It certainly wouldn't hurt," the lady said with a wink.

"No indeed," the parson replied, "it would improve my status among the ladies."

"Of that you have plenty as it is. But that's not what counts among women. Not status!"

Serious Mrs. Dvihally was accustomed to seeing her friend converse so casually with even the most unfamiliar men, but this was going rather far for her.

"How is the venerable wife faring?" she asked gravely.

"Thank you," the old parson responded in a cooler tone, then added peevishly: "She's suffering with her gout."

"In due time, we'll be doing the same!" the lady of the house laughed out loud.

"You shall never become an old woman!" the parson countered.

"I hope not."

"God forbid, my wife, an old woman!" her husband cried from the front room, as though he'd been listening in on them. "I'll bring the glasses in there, as us two out here won't manage to drink up these spirits by our lonesome."

Dvihally's wife regarded her husband anxiously. The slender, somber man stepped sedately into the drawing room and seated himself on a hard chair away from the others. His wife knew that he had for some time been interested in her female friend, but now she saw with amazement that he was making no secret of his ill humor and jealousy. The poor, downtrodden woman knew that he would now be morose for days, and she crossed herself. *Dear God*, she sighed from the bottom of her soul, *five children is a great many! What will I do if a sixth comes along ...*

The lady of the house was as lively as quicksilver. Her eyes twinkled, her face gleamed, she was more sparkling than at any time in her life. She knew how to captivate all her admirers at once and felt herself so rich that she could use this one afternoon to compensate for her entire life!

She would be able to look on this day with the happy feeling that there had been a time when half a dozen men battled for a mere look from her.

While they waged a cheerful war of rivaling mockeries with one another, an awkward young girl suddenly appeared. She was an underdeveloped girl of fifteen years, whose blotchy, pink complexion turned flaming red the moment she spied the large group, and her little eyes blinked nervously, like those of a captured bird.

"Ah, Marica, little Marica!" cried the lady of the house. "What have you got, dear Marica? How are your parents doing?"

The lady rose and rushed over to the girl, who stood in the door and said fearfully and so quietly that Mrs. Veres could barely understand her words: "Mama sent me here to ask if you would be so kind as to start the crochet-work off, I don't know how to work the stitch ..."

She spoke so anxiously and looked up into her face with such desperation that it made the lady laugh, upon which she gently placed her arm around the girl's waist and led her into the front room. There she positioned herself in front of the window and, as night was falling fast, strained her eyes to inspect the pattern.

"Dear child, it's quite simple," she said, her voice conveying the solace of the experienced expert who knew there was no need to be so nervous around men, who certainly didn't present the danger the girl's tousled little head led her to believe. In that moment the young girl forgot her discomfiture and nervousness and listened with understanding to the lady's explanations. In no time she understood the crochet pattern, as she was a teachable girl and a minute later knew exactly what she had to do.

"Thank you," she said and turned immediately, leaving so quickly it was as though she hadn't even been there. The teacher's wife looked after her rather gloomily – the child's indifference bothered her. The girl's lack of respect did not escape her notice. Much as the entire sea was somehow present in a single drop of water, all the arrogance of the small town aristocracy came through in this one small girl. That arrogance that was brimming with all the bitterness and saltiness of seawater, causing whoever tasted of it to pucker their lips in disgust. This child's father was merely a manorial understeward, but the family was possessed of the same highborn spirit as the duke himself. This girl knew she was lowering herself to run over to the teacher's wife and grant her the distinction of serving her as a consultant regarding her crochet work. She could have figured it out for herself, but why go to such lengths when this was simpler.

How fortunate for her! She herself was, after all, only the teacher's wife. And if twenty men were to run after her, it would do nothing to increase her prestige. On the contrary, it would tend to diminish it. People would consider her easy. *The scoundrels!* she said to herself, suddenly glowering spitefully after the girl. Of course, no one would give people such as them a second look. Her mother's face resembled that of a hairy ape. No man apart from her husband ever dared lay eyes on it. And yet, in that moment, she was bitterly envious, as that woman belonged to the upper social echelon of this town and would not even reciprocate her visit! ... That was the most frightful of insults in small-town society and could never be forgotten. It granted her minimal satisfaction that she herself had failed to reciprocate the visits of a few young couples. Unfortunately they belonged only to the better families of the merchant class, but she eagerly awaited the day when she could snub a true lady from the aristocracy in this way. She stood in the window, clenched her teeth, and stared out at the church. In one short moment her mood deteriorated to the point where she barely knew herself. She would have liked to throw the entire company out onto the street, then sit on the sofa and weep and weep. Bitterly.

She heard footsteps behind her – the floorboards creaked. Immediately she thought it was the parson coming. And indeed it was.

"Ah, my little lamb ... what are you doing here?"

She quickly dried her eyes with her handkerchief, then turned her shattered, pale face toward him.

"My God! Has something happened?" the parson asked in astonishment.

"No."

"My dear child," the parson said, then fell silent. Deeply troubled, he stared at length at the lady, who at first looked directly into his eyes, then turned her gaze from him.

"My dear child," the parson mumbled again, and his voice grided from the force of his blood as it began to churn. He grew bleary-eyed and, through this watery veil, he saw his most intimate desires approach the realm of the possible.

The failure of the lady to respond struck him as encouragement, and he quickly spoke: "If you, if you knew, if I could venture to say that ... dear child. If you would care to make an old man happy ... in strict confidence!" he said, swallowing hard. "The laws of God and of man, the laws of morality, and yet it's the heart that comes first. One can govern everything, but not that. Why do you subject yourself to pointless torment, my God, confess your grief to me, dear child, a compassionate heart ... Who here understands you, if they were to understand you, they would need the necessary life experience, and must love you to the extent of risking everything. I would enter into retirement, if ... My dear child, I worship you!"

The lady paid no attention to his stammering drivel, but this word slapped her brutally in the face. "You are insane!" she snapped gruffly at the old man.

At first he had no idea what to do, and he grabbed the lady's hand imploringly.

"Disgusting old ass!" the lady shouted, tearing his hand away.

The parson stared at her, his face chalk-white, his mouth hanging open. His rotten, jagged teeth protruded from his purple gums, and his lower lip hung down, trembling like that of a sobbing toddler. It took several minutes for him to regain his composure, and his blood then quickly cooled down as he recognized the danger that menaced him. What if someone had heard the lady's words!

"What must you think of me!" he stammered with the unabashed intent of shifting the blame for the situation from himself.

"That you are a nasty old pig!" the lady said, pleased for this opportunity to attack, harshly and openly, someone who occupied a much higher status than she, who was in every way her social superior.

The parson clasped his two hands together in horror. With one twitch of his eyes he begged for mercy, with the next he bid her silent.

The lady wasted no more time on him. She inserted herself even farther beneath the arched window and looked out at the sky.

The old man, who never in his life had been so thoroughly rebuffed and simply could not believe that the golden days when the teachers' wives thought it an honor for him to bestow his favor upon them were now gone, slowly began to comprehend what had happened to him.

"See here," he gasped in threatening proximity to her, his mouth reeking of tobacco, "should you want to say a word of this to anyone, I'll see to it myself that your nephew is thrown out of school, even if no one else does!"

The lady turned toward him with a look of contempt. "You?" she said, using a rudely familiar form of address.

"You! How dare you speak to me like that!"

"Disgusting old fool."

"So you prefer the younger ones? Huh? The little curate! No? Too bad, the young gentleman is departing from here tomorrow! But before that he'll have to admit what the two of you were doing last night! Otherwise I will rescind his diploma!"

"I'll have yours rescinded if you don't shut your mouth!"

The parson seethed over her vulgar tone. He knew it was just the usual gibberish, but he was losing his self-control, and in any case he was much less refined than his manner suggested in moments of calm, so he replied with:

"It's truly a fine thing when a married lady surrounds herself with suitors!"

"Old billy goat!" the lady responded in utter disgust, and turning away she added: "As though I would let a toad jump on me."

"By your leave, madam!" the parson crowed, and sought to leave in order to prevent a truly scandalous altercation.

But in that moment the curate appeared. Of course he had taken no part in the conversation occurring in the drawing room, his only thought had been of the lady, and in spite of his suspicion that his head was playing tricks on him, he felt he had to disrupt his superior's private encounter with the beautiful lady.

"Yes, curate sir?" the parson addressed him frostily.

"At your service!"

"Leave this room immediately!"

"If you please, sir ..."

"Not another word. I'll have you before the consistory. I heard what happened."

"Please, sir ..." the curate stammered, his face suddenly grown pale.

"You see? You see?" the parson said and turned his eyes toward the lady. "I'll send him away. Do you understand? We will leave this place!"

The lady shrugged her shoulder in the most ordinary fashion, like a servant.

"Go then ... up the white horse's ass!" she said, laughing over her own witticism. It was as though she could hear her father's voice ringing in her ears, who countless times had wished everyone from his wife to the emperor to this very same place. It felt good to behave precisely as her father used to – like a true daughter of the ancient Koppány[5] dynasty!

The parson could not speak another word. This scene was so base, so ugly, and so vulgar that it was too much even for him. He barked at the curate, who opened the door without further ado. They left.

The entire heated scene had caused barely any alarm in the large, low-vaulted room which was filled to the brim with furniture. It was almost a shame that the confrontation had been dampened so, at least in the noise it caused if not in the vehemence of its emotions. It somehow suited the white-masoned, medieval old edifice, that the walls should be renewed by this reminder of the ancient, fervent passions of men.

The lady looked after them, then turned away with flaming face. She went into the drawing room where her husband was explaining to the deputy judge how the peasants mixed carbon black in with the whitewash and used it to paint a strip along the bottom of their houses. But only the Hungarians did that, the Slovaks mixed washing blue into their whitewash, making it quite easy to know what sort of people were living in which house.

---

[5] A member of the royal Árpád dynasty of Hungary, Duke of Somogy County in the latter part of the tenth century.

"Where did the holy father go?" Mrs. Dvihally asked the lady of the house in a gently cooing tone as she entered the room.

The teacher's wife furrowed her brow and glared angrily at her. She saw that no one had heard a shred of the scene from before, except that this woman had seen everything from her vantage point across from the opening in the door. All of a sudden she hated her to the core, her hatred burst forth from her like pus from a punctured wound.

But she merely bit her lip and, feigning cheerfulness, laughed in the deputy judge's face.

"Did the parson leave?" the man of the house asked.

"Both of them," Mrs. Dvihally said quietly.

"What the deuce!" the man of the house said, springing to his feet. "Did they lose their minds?"

"Why do you involve yourself in others' affairs?" Dvihally asked his wife grimly.

The haggard, ill-tempered woman merely turned up her mouth. "I didn't involve myself. It's all the same to me. For all I care they can leave. I won't be running after them, that's certain."

"That's a shame, dear, a little exercise wouldn't hurt you!" the lady of the house said with malice.

"I see that it isn't doing someone else any good."

The lady of the house fixed her eyes on her guest and looked her up and down, as though she wanted to say: "Oh, you wretched thing, do you really want to start something with me?" She smiled at her, her face exuding contempt.

The deputy judge had no idea what was happening.

The other two men listened, each acting as if he didn't truly know that some sort of war between Amazons was about to break out. Veres rose apologetically, hoping to keep the peace.

"So, my dear, shouldn't I go after the two reverends?"

"It would be good for us to go after them!" Mrs. Dvihally said in a tearful tone.

"What in God's name is wrong with you!" her husband snapped at her. "Suddenly the women have gone insane."

"Hahaha!" Veres laughed out loud, as though this would make everything all right again. "It's true that, when it comes to women, one can never know when something will happen with them! Yes, for the poor man it's like walking along the rim of a volcano, he never knows when an explosion will go off beneath his feet."

The deputy judge withdrew even farther into the sofa corner where he'd taken refuge in the descending dark of evening from these emotionally volatile people.

"Let's go home," Mrs. Dvihally said as she rose to her feet, all but staggering.

"Sit back down. Have you lost your head? Confound it!" Dvihally grumbled.

"Come home. Just get away from here!" his wife choked tearfully.

"Damn it! You could maintain a bit of decorum."

"Decorum! Hahaha! That would be good … Let's go home now, old man!"

"What's the matter with you?" the lady of the house asked in a frighteningly sharp tone.

"Nothing, dear, I've just had enough of this visit for one afternoon."

"I hope not just for this one afternoon!"

"I hope the same!"

The lady of the house again fell silent. She didn't know what to do with the woman. Ideally she would have grabbed her friend by the throat and flung her out of the room.

"Phew! Phew!" Mrs. Dvihally gasped, "I can no longer bear the air in here."

"Well go to the deuce then! Who asked you to come here?"

"Your little heart!" the lady of the house said spitefully, as she had begun to suspect that jealousy had driven the sourpuss here, since she generally never left her home.

"No doubt! No doubt! But I greatly regret that I saw what I saw. In all truth, had my heart not led me here, God knows what would have happened …"

It was clear to everyone that the most bitter insult lurked within those harshly spoken words. Dvihally stood up and grabbed his wife by the arm.

"Go home if you're unhappy!" he yelled at her, his voice quaking with anger.

"Only if you come as well!"

"I? Well! ... Have a care!"

The lady of the house spoke with scorn: "Oh, let the old gaffer go as well. Good-bye! It was a pleasure having you."

Dvihally stopped short and fixed his gaze on the lady's gold tooth, which twinkled in the dim light. Then he sobered up and pulled himself together. He carried himself stiffly, like a hard rubber ball void of air, with only the stiffness of the material to give it its form.

He turned around in silence, went into the front room, took his hat and walking stick, and departed frostily, without saying goodbye, through the low front door.

His wife followed him, amidst profuse and poorly concealed sobbing.

"If you'd known, if you'd seen," she sniveled, "oh, old friend, my God, my God ..."

Pál Veres thought to himself for a moment, then after a brief inner struggle left his wife and quickly followed after them – his creaking footsteps on the stairs still audible after he'd closed the door behind him. Then his voice could be heard in the courtyard as he called after the Dvihallys: "Wait friends, please, I'll accompany you home."

The deputy judge felt a wave of heat pass through him. His hands began to shake, his knees trembled, as a torrid sensation coursed through his body in great waves.

He was alone with the lady and in that moment he disregarded the strange, incomprehensible altercation that had taken place before his eyes, as the feverish knowledge that they were alone there aroused him.

He sought to stand up, to spring to his feet. He knew that the lady truly beonged to him now. He could pluck her. Embrace her. This ripe fruit ready to fall from the tree.

And his hand quivered on the arm of the sofa and he stroked the worn plush upholstery, massaging it with a gentle touch, as though it were the lady's flesh.

But why did he not jump up, why not leap at his prey, which trembled at him with flaring heat.

And it was dark. The glowworm light of the street lamps now shone outside and the wan yellow luster lit the lady's face. And the lady just stood, and waited. Her eyes peered motionlessly into the light ...

Finally the young man dared to move, the creaking of the sofa springs beneath him gave him courage.

He rose and closed in on her, with calculated deliberation, every step like a mile in the blazing sun. And the more he saw, knew, that every resistance, every struggle on the part of the lady was transformed into surrender, the bolder, stronger, and more purposeful he became.

He stretched forth his hand and grabbed the lady with a quick, cunning, audacious thrust. He grasped her arms, her two tautly fleshed, nicely plumped arms, and he twitched with heat, as though an electric battery had stimulated him.

And the lady closed her eyes and relaxed her arms, took stock of the world and was without fear of what might happen next ...

The man's kissing lips sank into the lady's dense hair, he embraced her ecstatically and his handsome face glid down across her forehead, her eyes, her burning mouth, which pined with fervor, with lust, with the torpid yearning of long, long unfulfilled desire.

And then the door opened in the front room. Glaring light filled the space, yet they could hardly bear to disentangle themselves.

The man sank down in his former spot. The lady leaned back against the table.

Her back was to the door when Laci entered with a brightly lit lamp.

The youth's eyes burned. He knew what he'd done. All afternoon he'd eavesdropped on what was going on in there and had seen the departure of the parson with the curate, of the Dvihallys, and then his father. He was horrified to see who remained and what was transpiring between them. He all but tortured his brain to come up with a reason to enter the room. And when he thought of the lamp, he rushed into the kitchen and broke the smaller table lamp they were accustomed to using. The large one was the one he must light.

"I kiss your hand! Good evening!" he said, his voice shaking.

The lady looked back at him and blinked her eyes repeatedly as a means of cloaking her inward trembling.

The youth placed the lamp on the table and stood there.

"Have a seat, Laci!" the lady said dryly, unaware that she'd used a more formal form of address with him, as though he were a stranger.

With that she went to the window, opened it nervously, and leaned out. She rested her face on her palms, and blue and red rings danced before her eyes. Slowly they formed into an intense, small point of light, and she strained her vision from behind closed lids to make out the outlines of this image. It was the lamp. Yes indeed, a tiny little lamp.

Then she thought how her husband would soon be returning home. Angrily she said to herself: *It's good at least to have a husband, someone with whom I can't get caught ...*

She clenched her teeth and spread her lips apart in her torment.

She wanted to bite someone.

But she merely groaned and waited for everyone to leave so she could be alone with her husband.

She furrowed her brow and thought with stern dominance and commanding desire of her own, unique and wretched husband.

XI

For some time, not a single word was spoken. The student sat down stubbornly in an armchair, his forehead wrinkled and his cheekbones protruding stiffly through his fleshless skin. The deputy judge was overcome with languor after his intense and unsatisfied arousal, and he sank back down into the corner of the sofa. He closed his eyes for a few moments and felt as though he could fall asleep. Then he stared at the lady, who was leaning out the window, her narrow skirt pressed across her thighs; the harsh light of the lamp outlined a powerfully malleable nude even amidst the shadows it cast. The young man's blood renewed its stirring and his spine tingled painfully in his lust. He eyed the student with hatred, his eyes flashing from his motionless face.

His gaze met that of the youth, and he was ashamed of himself. He saw how the boy sat beside him full of spite, like a eunuch. He loured at him and clenched his teeth in disgust. This entire little town was simply repulsive. He was here for the first time in his life today. And today he was unable to achieve everything he could with a woman solely because an entire raft of minions suddenly emerged to engage, like him, in mutual leering and dread.

This meat market struck him as so cheap that the stench made his nose wrinkle. *What a base, dishonest, immoral, abhorrent, bad group of people!* he cursed to himself. And he was glad that he occupied a distant sphere from these people, he was glad that he had not become a part of this chaff. Now he risked becoming the object of his own loathing. For he sensed that, as pleasurable as the satisfaction of his sudden desire might have been, profound and painful revulsion would have remained in its wake. Wherein lay the value of such meager joy. How many predecessors must have gone before him if the job was so easily accomplished ...

He would have liked to be far from this place. As though the air he was breathing would contaminate him. He longed for some clean, fine sensation, and he thought of the notary's wife.

He turned his head to keep from seeing the form of the teacher's wife and, with eyes closed, tried to conjure up the small, elegant, delicate figure of the notary's wife in the light that filtered through his eyelids. He heard her pleasant, clever little voice, tried to imagine the smell of her perfume, and even managed to picture her sparkling blue eyes for one brief moment. How different the atmosphere was there. The refined atmosphere of intellectual company held sway there, with more elevated topics, sophisticated style, a harmonious ambience, a tone conducive to conversations as opposed to sensations.

He would go there. He hadn't seen the genteel lady in quite a long time. Yet she always received him warmly. Poor dear, she had next to no company in this barbaric world where no one managed to rise above the peasant sphere. Her husband was a prettified man, fastidious and sprucely attired, like a notary from a French comedy, and as boorish as the most common of Ilosva peasants. He must go immediately to this woman – he thirsted for her as the consumptive thirsts for fresh forest air.

Creaking, clopping sounds were heard. The teacher burst in with eagle eyes, unable to suppress his fear and suspicion.

Once he laid eyes on the silent group, he quickly relaxed. His face blazed like a lantern and he broke forth with his war cry: "By George! What sort of a host am I! Well, two young men ought to be able to amuse a woman! What did I miss?"

The little lady looked from the window into the well-lit room and, straightening herself, turned back toward the night.

Not a soul responded to the man of the house's alarm.

"Well, let's just take up where we left off! New glasses for all, madam hostess!"

"Pardon me, teacher sir," the deputy judge said, rising wearily to his feet, "but I must leave."

"Of course that's out of the question! We'll have none of that, judge sir!"

But the deputy judge stood determinedly, waiting for the stream of words gushing forth from the teacher to end.

"Of course you can't leave, not now of all things! We're about to live it up like kings! I can't help it if some quitter jumped ship like a rat for reasons that are anybody's guess. We aren't like that! Right? Of course not!"

"Without a doubt," the deputy judge replied, "but there's something I have to do ..."

"At nine in the evening?"

"Yes, well, I wasn't aware that I would receive such a thoughtful ... uh ... invitation. I already agreed to go yesterday ... and now I must leave ..."

He was so incredibly flustered that he had no idea what he was saying and knew even less what words he should use.

"It's a shame, truly a shame," the teacher chattered. "I can say, with a pure heart I can truly say that it's a great shame, judge sir, there's no need to be so obstinate, like a mule ... that is to say, well see here, I'm only saying what's on my mind ... I mean, what my mouth babbles forth."

"By your leave, teacher sir – I sincerely appreciate the invitation. I'm sorry I didn't have the opportunity, regarding what we discussed, nor will it present itself in future. There's really no need for me to interfere. The young gentleman is quite an upstanding, tactful youth, there's nothing to fear, I'm convinced the faculty knows him well and won't make an issue of such a petty affair."

The student rose and took in the deputy judge's graciously condescending words, his face blood red. The lady hadn't turned back from the window, but she listened and began to suspect something, she knew not what.

"By your leave, teacher sir!" the deputy judge said, extending his hand with a gesture that expressed his firm determination to turn his back on this entire household.

"I kiss your hand, gracious lady!" he said, bowing in the direction of the window.

"Good day!" the lady turned and said. Her face was cold and arrogant, almost contorted with rigidity. She refused to extend her hand.

The young man was insulted and grew flustered. This he wasn't prepared for. For them to throw him out!

"Gracious lady!" he said, unable to avoid feeling offended, "I'm very glad that I could spend the afternoon in your honorable company."

The lady looked him up and down with cold, contemptuous, scornful, mocking eyes, her lips expressing extreme disdain, and refused to acknowledge his response.

The young man blushed from head to toe, his entire body turning red, and he bowed like a doomed man who has mounted the scaffold.

He turned around numbly and left.

The teacher followed him.

The student remained where he was, not daring to look up. As the teacher showed the deputy judge to the door, evidently with the intention of assuaging him, the student still did not move a muscle.

The lady approached him with silent, swaying steps, and saw that the youth was trembling as though a mesmerist were advancing toward him.

A small teardrop appeared in the lady's eye, and with a bold and desperate movement she came very near to him, all but snuggling against him, then looked up at him – her eyes were on a slightly lower level than his – and compelled the boy to direct his tearful, trembling gaze into her own.

The youth opened his mouth, but his lower jaw only twitched, two or three times in a row, his throat emitting no sound.

The lady smiled gently, kindly, understandingly, empathetically, encouragingly into his face, and with that the youth said quickly, with a nervous stutter: "I wish you a good night."

The lady smiled warmly at him. Never before had she felt such a pleasant sensation of motherly innocence.

"Good night, Laci!" she said, raising her hand to caress the youth's face. First she traveled with her left hand from his hair to his chin, then with her right. She proceeded to hold his face in her two hands as though she were drawing water from a spring, and then she performed a great work of charity: she offered her mouth for him to kiss, softly, tearfully, and the youth touched her lips with his, like a child. In that moment the lady shuddered and, with an energetic thrust, grabbed the youth's face in her soft hands, and planted a savage, fiery, noisy kiss in the plump nest of his boyish lips.

Then she released him and quickly returned to the window. "Good night," she said, "good night."

Rainbow colors flitted before the youth's eyes, he shivered over his entire body, as though he were suffering from a cold fever. He managed to perceive his aunt indicating that he should go. She waved at him. He took it as a command. He turned and left with tentative steps.

The lady waited until the youth's steps were audible from the other room. With heightened awareness, she listened to the sound of his footsteps. She heard as he closed the door at the end of the hall behind him and believed with pleasure that she could hear the boy fling himself sobbing onto his bed. And then all the bitterness in her life suddenly erupted and she threw herself onto the sofa and wept.

She'd finished crying by the time her husband returned home.

The man was smoking moodily, and as he set down his cigar he proceeded to bite his lips. His great moustache hung down and his eyebrows twitched so crossly it seemed they not only sensed but sought to reveal his sullenness.

"Oh my, oh my," he sighed repeatedly, and bustled distractedly about the room. He didn't even glance at his wife. He saw that she'd been crying and said to himself: "Now you're sobbing. After you've ruined everything. Lightning should strike all you women. You're so impudent. Just when things are going well, you go stark raving mad. Then you cry."

He'd felt the humiliation to which the deputy judge had subjected him, who'd rebuffed him icily, hostilely, almost crudely in the street. It had angered him that Veres had accompanied him all the way to the notary's door. Veres knew that he would never again socialize with him, but he thought: *It is a long lane that has no turning, things can't help but get better*. Soon he would repay him for his rudeness. Should he likewise send him packing? Break off all relations with him? ... Now he was certain he must stir up the people against the mayor. He could already see himself pacing excitedly up and down the room as he met with the citizens of the town, orating against the notables. The old scoundrel would cease to be mayor in this town. Just let them get past this year!

The mayor was the teacher's last resort. Whatever bitter experience might befall him, his ultimate aim was exacting revenge on the mayor.

"Of course – my wife is right! He'll marry the mayor's daughter. Good – but we'll turn the heat up on the papa before the wedding. Maybe he won't marry the daughter if we oust the old codger from office.

Amidst his confused musings, he also thought that that would also result in revenge against the deputy judge if he spoiled his lust for the mayor's daughter.

"Well, get the beds ready, then we'll go to sleep," he said as though, having reached the end of a typical day, it was the most natural thing in the world for a man to go to bed.

The lady didn't move.

The teacher continued pacing back and forth, but even his desire to do that had waned. He scratched his nose and sought something with which to distract himself. He was already sick of all the rancor, he would have liked to turn his thoughts to more run-of-the-mill matters. It occurred to him what a nice matter it would be now if he had never gotten married. His bed would long since have been readied, he would lie down, sleep, and when he got up in the morning, he would have to think at length regarding what had gotten him so upset yesterday. That is, the devil would have to think about it! Who will bother thinking about what was so upsetting yesterday! It's best to forget such things immediately.

"So, aren't we going to bed?"

The lady looked up. Scornfully.

"Well, if you aren't tired yet! ...," the husband added.

"Go and lie down!" The lady's tone was cruel, stern and harsh. Her voice was as though transformed.

The teacher wrenched his neck and turned up his mouth. Then he stood in front of the window and began to carefully twist his moustache, twirling it with both hands, like a cat washing itself. He even purred, humming some song or other.

"You shouldn't have married!" said the woman bitterly.

The man raised his eyebrows and looked out at the street lamp, which now looked like it was flickering.

"But even more importantly, I shouldn't have married *you*!"

The lady raised herself from her half-prone position. "Oh, God! Belated regret! I should have foreseen it!"

She rose, intending to leave, but then she sat back down and stared frozenly into space. She placed her hand over her stomach, which was twisted in knots. She bent over herself. "You're a scoundrel too for having married me."

The teacher started agitatedly at this strong language.

"Wretched scoundrel."

The man decided not to put up with this, but he merely heaved a sigh and scratched his head.

"I would just like to know why you married me!" She looked over at him, waiting for a response. "Well? Such a wretch! Such a nobody! How could you dare marry a young creature!"

The teacher felt as though dust were being stirred up in his face, and rubbed his eyes.

"Scoundrel. What would you say if I cheated on you! ... If I weren't an honorable woman ... I could have done it a hundred times over. I've certainly good reason. God himself, even he couldn't fault me for it."

The husband shifted his weight from one leg to the other. He felt terrible. He was ashamed of himself and didn't dare utter a response.

"Do you hear what I'm saying?" she screamed with a sickly groan and bent over herself even harder as her cramps intensified. Saliva pooled in her mouth and sweat accumulated on her forehead.

"I'm not deaf."

"Answer, then!"

"With what?"

"How you could dare to make me unhappy my entire life long!?"

"Why are you unhappy?"

"Why? ..."

"It strikes me that your entire existence consists solely of amusement. Name just one woman in the entire town who amuses herself as much as you do."

"Splendid."

"Are we not anywhere and everywhere? If actors come to town, we attend every performance. If some entertainment takes place, we're never absent."

"Except from the ball of the elites."

"Yes, well, since I'm not a member of that company! But otherwise we go to everything. And nearly every day, either we're visiting someone else or they're visiting us. I don't even know when we've gone to bed this early. That's why I'm so sleepy now. It's true, I'm no longer young enough. I can barely keep my eyes open."

"Miserable, shiftless scoundrel," the lady gasped, groaning in pain – her innards writhed in torment.

"Look here, little mother, let's just go to bed nicely – then tomorrow we can talk everything over."

The wife got up, her pain having suddenly ended, and rushed to take advantage of the time she had before her colic or whatever the devil it was resumed, and she passed through the front room into her bedroom. She lit a candle and began to ready her bed. She disrobed immediately. Meanwhile, she extinguished the candle. She sat down on the edge of the bed, cried, buried herself in the covers, and sprawled herself out there like an invalid.

She was exhausted, she felt her eyelids quickly grow heavy, and fell asleep, her mouth hanging open.

She didn't even notice as her husband stole into the dark room and wasted no time lying down to sleep.

After a long, stuporous rest, she awoke after midnight, but in the first few minutes she was still dazed and didn't know what sound she'd heard, some unaccustomed din; as her thoughts cleared, whatever it was that had attracted her attention as she'd awoken left her mind.

Her sleepiness melted away. In fact, she felt as fresh as ever. Her body was suddenly so awake that she felt like a young girl. She was covered only with a thin linen sheet, and even that felt like too much. It was as black as pitch. Her husband snorted on the other bed in the back of the room – the two beds stood end-to-end alongside the wall. A wave of heat passed through her body, which seemed to smolder. She must remove her covers. As her hand moved across her skin, her sensuality blazed forth.

"I'm so beautiful," she whispered to herself rapturously, "and no one will ever appreciate it. My body is so comely! Every detail is beautiful. And yet withered Mrs. Dvihally gets more out of her life than I, even today ..."

She petted herself across her entire body, with loving strokes, then suddenly all the bitterness that had gnawed at her in the evening, exhausting her and sapping her strength, burst forth with renewed intensity.

"I'm suffering for my sins! I am damned. I sold myself. What could I expect at the age of twenty-four from a much older man. A poor girl, the entire world's foot rag, for everone to wipe their filthy boots with. Of course there was the inevitable enslavement in duty, as in a prison, in the midst of torment. That, too, was a way to escape! ... One thinks one's life is blossoming, and hell ... But my face is no longer pretty. I'm not a fresh young girl any more.

Wrinkles surround my eyes. When I sleep poorly, the next day I look like a hag. But my body was never so beautiful! So strong, so voluptuous. How white I am! Other women my age all have lumpy, wrinkled paunches, like sacks full of potatoes. Their legs are covered with gnarled streaks, like grilled chicken. And they whine and snivel, and can't even climb a hill, they coat their backs with salve and complain when their husbands touch them. Oh, how I would wrestle them – I'd break the bones of any man I embraced!"

She flung herself down onto the bed and stretched herself out.

She writhed for several minutes and thrashed her burning body about on the hot matress.

"Laci, dear! Little man!" she suddenly whispered into the pillow, and again: "Laci, dear! My little lover!"

She was certain her husband was awake on the other bed. His snoring and snorting had ceased, and he breathed evenly, yet deeply.

"The wretch is pretending to sleep."

And that roused her to dizzying anger.

"No, that's not how it works, teacher sir! That I should put up with that for long! I, too, am a human being, daughter of Mary, no saint! Twice you escaped shame. Thanks to my stupidity, and to that wicked boy! ..."

She pressed her teeth together and sensed how some great, momentous decision was filling, flooding her. It paralyzed her entire body. For several moments her powers of thinking ceased, then this notion took complete control of her. She relinquished herself to it. As of yet she was incapable of carrying it out, yet she felt as though she already had. The fever of the decision quickly stormed through her, leaving only its accomplishment to continue seething in her veins.

Her living widowhood was at an end. Now she would get up and go out, let this man just try to stand in her way! The man who was lying there, so near, whose head she could kick and who was pretending to sleep.

Her thoughts were bestial and narrowly circumscribed by their primitive nature, but her physical powers were unbelievably capacious.

Inwardly she felt terribly faint. And yet it was precisely her weakness that gave her the strength she needed to rouse herself, to rise up and take flight. It didn't worry her that the floorboard creaked beneath her feet. Nor that the key grated in the unoiled lock, or that a draft pushed the door shut as she again reached for the handle.

Feverishly, almost deliriously, she moved along the cold floor tiles and grasped the iron door handle to the student's room like a feverish invalid grasps the cold spoon: whatever is in it must be swallowed.

She stepped into the room. She stood just inside the door. The moon gleamed through the window and her chemise shone white.

Not a sound. Oh, the sweet child. The dear boy. He's sleeping. He doesn't awaken. She waited a few moments so as not to alarm him. Then she smiled. Poor boy. Should he wake up now, he'll see a ghost and scream! And his desire to make love will leave him.

Overcome with feminine compassion, she pitied the innocent, virgin boy, and in a sudden impulse it became clear to her what she must do. With trembling hands she reached toward her shoulders and undid the two buttons!

After that she stood there like a fairy. In the yellow, secretive glow of the moon. And she knew that her body shone like a radiant light source, and that beams of fiery light shot forth from her heart with every beat.

And yet the silence remained unbroken.

She can no longer bear it. She closes her eyes and whispers: "Laci!"

Then in a louder, more anxious, more promising tone: "Laci!"

Dazzling silence.

Fearful anxiety takes hold of her.

"Laci!" she cries, rushing toward his bed.

The bed is empty. And the room is likewise empty. And the bird has flown far, far away.

And as she sinks onto the bed, giddy from the huge rush of blood that has coursed through her body, she knows clearly, surely, with deathly certainty where the boy is.

She'd awoken as he'd left.

When he'd left the building and gone out into the night. In order to break his great piece of gold up into small change! That large chunk of sensual gold that she'd pressed onto his lips during the evening.

She lies there for a long time, to the point of perhaps even losing consciousness.

After an hour, she awakens languidly, ailing. Again she is overcome by cramps, as during the evening. She has to crouch down on the floor, suddenly shaking with fever and chills. Feverish pangs flash painfully through her body, over her face, across her forehead. Nausea overcomes her and she feels abject and miserable.

She has to wait for the attack to pass from her, at which point she gropes her way to her feet and looks for her chemise. She's frightfully bitter and unable even to appreciate her good fortune in not losing her virtue in the course of her delirium. Her true character comes over her and from somewhere in her heart prayerful gratitude bubbles forth: as though the hand of God had watched over her, removing from her the chance to sin. Suddenly her physical pain subsides completely, as though it had never been, and she flees from the room, feeling fresh and happy. But no sooner do her feet contact the cold tile floor of the hallway than the pain seizes her with renewed force, the cramps return to her innards, forcing her to fall to a squat once more. She groans and quakes, and weeps.

When her anguish abates somewhat, she calculates where she can find a jigger of brandy while making the least noise possible. There is rum in the kitchen.

She gropes her way into the kitchen, finds the bottle and drinks. It only makes her feel worse, she has to sit down. She's convinced she's about to die.

She has no idea how she made it into bed. She's barely able to suppress her groans, she lies there overcome with illness.

Soon she falls asleep – even her desire to keep watch on her husband as he stirs and sighs can't keep her awake.

Dawn is well underway as she awakens. Her husband is gone from the room.

As she turns in her bed, she senses something cold sticking to her thigh, and she's so weak she can hardly move.

"Ah, now I know what was wrong with me," she says, reckoning what day of the month it is. "Aren't I fortunate," she adds, smiling bitterly. "Just what I would need, another child to deal with. How we would look then!"

Again she falls asleep from her weakness and the great loss of blood. She gets up around noon.

When she gets dressed and drags herself over to the mirror like an autumn fly, she's too drained even to react in horror at what she sees there.

A thoroughly aged woman's face stares back at her from the mirror. Dark shadows surround her eyes, deep furrows edge the sides of her mouth, her neck sags, and a prominent depression occupies the space between her collar bones.

"The novel is over!" she thought to herself, and she looked back on her youth, her happiness, her love life, like an old woman. Coolly, indifferently, without emotion, matter-of-factly: utter foolishness, all of it.

"No matter ... So much the better ... One can get over it that much sooner. At least now I understand what it means for a young woman to catch up in age with her older husband."

Her husband entered the room. He was lively and fresh, in a very good mood. His eyes sparkled and flashed about like twinkling fleas, and he eyed her face with a hint of guile.

"Well, little mother! ... Our boy Laci returned home from school. Aren't you curious regarding the outcome? ... What's wrong, then? You're not yourself at all ... By George."

The lady turned around and a tear rolled from her eye down across her face.

"What do you care what's wrong with me! ... Just be glad that things have gone well with you ... You've grown more youthful at my side ..."

XII

The residents of Víg's quarters filled the outer room to the headmaster's office.

Two doors were located to either side of the long, narrow outer office. The one led to the headmaster's office, the other to the professors' room. The boys listened beside the door on the right. The noise of the professors' discussion was audible from within. The investigation and interrogation had lasted well into yesterday evening, and now they'd been ordered to appear for the reading of the verdict.

Outside the weather was beautiful, with its angular rays the sun warmed the room where the boys stood like penned up sheep. A number of them bore desperate expressions. Szegő pressed his knees together, his limbs shaking badly out of fear, even though he was the only one there who had absolutely nothing to be afraid of. Mácsik, the little gentleman with the soft, red face who was guilty of some lewd transgression or other even when no one suspected it, was by contrast not the least bit affected.

"Why be such asses," he comforted the others, "the whole thing is just a lot of pompousness! They can't even punish us. Their problem in there is that they can't come up with the proper language to let us go. To hell with them."

The future judge affecting gravity came through in his mien; one could almost see how this pearl of lewdness would one day hold sway in the courtroom with a marble face. He gestured dismissively with his hand, then he thought of a prank. There at the opposite end of the outer office, beside the door to the hallway, stood the caretaker, whose duty it was to prevent the boys from listening in at the door.

"Uncle Berti!" Mácsik whispered.

The caretaker was accustomed from his days as a soldier to rush over immediately when addressed this way. Startled out of his passive pose, he responded: "How may I help you, sir?"

"Isn't it true that you're the one who lost the battle of Königgrätz[6]?"

"No, young man, I was at the camp in Olmütz then."

"Oh my, so *that's* why they lost the battle. I knew right away that you *must* have played some role in the affair."

The boys turned their backs on the room and looked out the window in order to avoid erupting in laughter. Even the caretaker smiled and shook his head.

---

[6] The loss of this battle in 1866 led to the defeat of the Austrian Empire, of which Hungary was a part, by Prussia.

After a time, Mácsik whispered to the boys: "Darn, if I'd thought of it, I would've brought the old man a couple good cigars!"

Then he said out loud: "Uncle Berti!"

"Hold still, young man!"

"Psst! I just wanted to tell you to be quiet!" – and he gestured impishly to that effect. Then he tiptoed over to the door to the professors' room and positioned his head in front of the keyhole. The caretaker raised his hand in dismay.

"Jiminy! Enough of your antics, young man!" He sprang over and sought to pull him away.

"What's the matter, Uncle Berti? I'm just listening!"

The boys hunched over against the wall, unable to contain their laughter. Even Kovács crouched down, as he couldn't control his laughing fit while standing. "Why, Uncle Berti, that's why I gave you three fancy cigars this morning!"

The laughter roared from all sides.

"Settle down, young man!" the injured caretaker groaned threateningly.

At that point a few sharp words were heard from the professors' room. No one understood them except Mácsik, who cheekily maintained his position at the door. The handsome young man made a long face and listened anxiously. But the caretaker no longer cared about the noise, he grabbed him by the arm and thrust him back among the others, then positioned himself in front of the door like a nice, chubby cherub.

"What was that, what was that?" the boys demanded of Mácsik.

"I didn't completely understand it. Someone came in and said that ... some lady or other was murdered."

"Please, she cheated on her husband!" Benedek's pointed, sanctimonious voice was heard. "But the Don Juan broke his neck as well!"

The boys looked at one another in amazement. Laci Veres's heart beat palpably. Had he not seen his uncle this morning calmly strolling about the courtyard, he would now have thought of him.

From within, they rang for the caretaker, who opened the door and stepped inside. The boys eavesdropped with taut nerves. The caretaker returned after one minute. He opened the door to the headmaster's office and ordered the youths harshly: "Please go inside!"

"Aha, they don't want us to hear anything!" Mácsik said.

The caretaker accompanied them inside. But now that they were that much farther away from the professors' ears, they began to speak more loudly.

"But who's the person who cheated on her husband! And who is the gentleman!" Mácsik exclaimed.

"My friend, it's the most awe-inspiring matter in the world," Kardos spoke in his coarse, surly voice. "Upon my honor!"

"Did the lady die? Didn't you hear?" asked Palotay, who was rather distracted. He ferretted about for information regarding where the incident could have occurred.

"I didn't hear."

"If someone murdered her, she must have died. Isn't that so?" Kardos spoke up.

"But who can it be!" several of them whispered, looking at each other in terror, as though Death with its foul, supernatural breath had entered their midst in order to examine them on future lessons and theories.

"Sadly, my friend," Palotay spoke with importance, "I can assure you that there is not a single lady in this town whose husband could not put her to death if that were the punishment for infidelity."

Some of the boys looked with envy at the tall, elegant youth. In school he always displayed a deplorable lack of knowledge, but they were all well aware that women didn't ask whether someone knew their way around aorist verb forms, rather they looked at the "impression" a man made.

They fell silent and everyone called forth the women he knew, one by one, and several of them considered with sweat-covered brow whether this one or that one hadn't come to grief at the hands of this or the other man.

Laci Veres stood wearily and sadly among the group, unable to pay attention to anything, sinking more and more deeply into himself; his head fell onto his chest and he neither saw nor heard a thing, only his own private thoughts clattered through his brain. He would have preferred it if they had thrown him out of school immediately. He felt like a sinner in love, as though he should take upon himself the punishment for every lady, every sinful woman. He was humbled and reviled, stripped of all his illusions. He thought of the night and bewept his idealism, his virginity. He felt tainted and feared he must succumb "to some illness." If only he'd stayed home, hadn't gone out during the night! ... if only some divine miracle had rescued him from the sinful, horror-filled night ... From disenchantment ... *That was all?!* – he repeated to himself – *that was love? for that women and men destroyed themselves? That was why the genders desired each other?* His entire world seemed to have fallen apart and turned to dust around him. Every one of his illusions was swept away. It was paradise lost! Recognition had demolished the paradise of his fantasy. He was sleepy, unbelievably sleepy, and still his brain was able to form ideas, and he came upon a magnificent discovery: the expression "paradise lost," and the biblical image of Adam and Eve as they lost their paradise over the knowledge they'd acquired, what had happened to him meant nothing other than that, only that. Now he too had lost his paradise, forever, irretrievably. What did the splendor beyond the gate mean to him now, that glory that had excited, had animated, occupied him so, from which he'd expected so much that he hardly dared to hope for its advent – henceforth he began to feel like a worm that must creep in the dust and eat dirt. And yet he believed that the woman was the sacrifice, and he the murderer. And he felt like he had, through that single contemptible deed, sinned against all womankind ... But after the moment of ecstasy it was as though the wind had blown away some heavy, oppressive fog, suddenly it had struck him that all women collectively constituted an empty, abject vessel toward which the male sex made its pilgrimage, overcome with thirst, and from which it received nothing but disgust instead of satisfaction. And he looked with aversion at those boys who all must have already lived through that same disillusionment that he was experiencing today, yet nonetheless were full of good cheer and excitement and aspired to things, lived, waited and sought. What, what? What followed death?

Apparently life followed death. Surely he, too, could become an ordinary, decent man, gone were the splendors, he no longer expects too much of anything ... He glanced around him. He looked at each person's face. With wide open eyes, as though he wanted now to come clean with the truth. And it occurred to him how last year, when his closest friend, his roommate Jenő, had gone one night down the same road he himself had just come from, the next day he'd looked into his face as though expecting something wondrous – how could the enormous transformation not be visible in his entire face, in his form, his very being! The awesome experience must have physically changed him: it must be stamped in undeniable signs into his physical being that, behold, this boy was now a man because he had united himself with a woman. And he thought of the grown student who for years had asserted in front of his own ears that he could tell from every girl's face whether she'd already experienced love and how often! Was there any more natural thing in all the world? And could there be anything more natural than that everyone should now point at him and that his disgusting accomplices should roar with laughter in his face and cry out to him: "Look, now you, too, belong with us!"

He shrank in on himself as he thought how pure from sin he'd been the day before, and then he skulked in shame to realize: now he was just as dirty and contaminated as the others. Oh, how little he would have appreciated yesterday in what glorious, angelic purity he'd lived! And with what ardent desire, how gladly he'd rushed onto the bridge of slaughter ...

It struck him that perhaps his justification might lie in this profound ignorance, as though that might excuse him from judgment, then the thought flashed across his mind: what did this bodily purity, preserved by him as much out of cowardice as out of chance, hailed by everyone as a source of pride, even mean? Now his soul was stained, even before he had any inkling regarding what he had defiled. How many battle-tested nights had he had! How many hundreds, how many thousands of sins against himself! He'd been a small boy, at most five years old, when he'd first played in his dreams with a little girl ... And he'd been a relatively big boy, a grammar school student, when he'd learned the truth that was as simple as all truths. To this day he was dazed with surprise by it. Mankind's origins struck him as so primitive, implausible and hideous, that he didn't dare believe it all. And he still didn't believe it. He beautified it, dressed it up, imagined it as an angelic and sacred splendor, as a herald of earthly majesty and repository of elysian pleasures ... And now, now he had to witness how badly the reality lagged behind the illusion ...

But this again brought him some degree of comfort. The vanity of his sense of self lent him support; only for these animals, these vacuous, soulless, uninspired mortals was true love such a precious commodity! But for him, who possessed such great imagination and wealth of feeling, it meant nothing. Where was the woman who was capable of instilling ardent ideas in him in the way that he himself was? Where the female he could fall in love with as easily as he could with his own self-conceived womanly ideal! ... Who could provide for him the same degree of sexual pleasure that he could conjure up for himself behind closed doors.

And he furrowed his brow; his haggard cheekbones projected conspicuously, and he stood there, skinny and pale, like a rabid dog. He was ready to bite others and to bite himself.

He ground his teeth and heaved a sigh, wishing he could bite the legs of Fate, who'd hurled him down to the ground to be the footrag of Life.

He heard nothing of what was going on around him. He stood leaning beside the window as though delirious. The boys sensed he was in dire straits and were afraid to try and comfort him. But he was already smiling, painfully, with the smile of patient oblivion, in his tired, dreamy rapture, as though he'd risen above arid, dusty human sobriety. It was all so unimportant to him, so terribly irrelevant, this worthless existence in which his every move was observed; where he was chastised, acquitted, called a liar, or let go with a slap on the wrist. He struggled against Life and the hope began to dawn in him that he might emerge victorious. What did he know about this victory, where or how it would be won: what he did know was that the lady was erased from his life, and that every goalpost which others had erected in the sort of incendiary faith that renders youth blind had crashed down in front him. He was repulsed by the dry land that gave mankind his footing, as it was muddy and dusty and covered with filth. And he longed for the ether, for some more refined region, where the gross, obese effluvium of the human mindset did not render him abject: the solid morals, the ethical consequentiality, the indefatigable industry ... For greater truths! Rarer successes! More exponential nervous splendors! Joy! Bliss! For reality kills. This life asphyxiates a person like muddy floodwaters, bearing carrion and excrement and the sewage of unknown cities. Let the amphibians gorge themselves in it, here he himself must drown. Drown!

He grabbed his throat and groaned out loud.

In that moment the door to the room opened. The headmaster entered, along with two professors.

The headmaster went to the table, and the boys stood there expectantly.

"My sons," the headmaster said in his petulant, non-oratorical manner. "The faculty council has reached an extraordinarily merciful and benevolent decision. We have before us an entire body of evidence from which it is clear that each and every one of you must have earned the harshest of punishments. Nonetheless, the honorable professors have heeded not your sins, but rather their own hearts. Which hearts have told them that young people at your age are extremely susceptible to such sins of the flesh and readily defy school rules. For this reason the honorable faculty council seeks to avoid suggesting to the world, precisely through punishment of the advanced grammar school students, those who are about to leave the school, that in this school of all places young people are being educated of whose morality one cannot assume with certainty that later, when it emerges in adult life, it will be able to respect the lofty moral commandments of humanity! My sons, I hereby inform you that the faculty council has condemned all of you to your deserved punishments and that they have sentenced one of you, you all know which one, to expulsion from all Hungarian schools ... But the faculty council has taken into consideration the fact that you, my young friends, have done what you did only out of ill-considered recklessness, and now the faculty council turns to you: place your hands over your hearts and state whether you are guilty. If you confess your offenses with honest and repentant hearts, then you will attain forgiveness. Do you confess?"

"We confess," the boys responded in eager chorus.

"Well then, I hereby proclaim in the name of the faculty council, that we shall no longer call you children, but rather young men, from whom we can henceforth expect that for the remaining days you spend within the walls of this institution, you shall conduct yourselves in an exemplary manner and thus, by your seriousness and your overall comportment, serve as models to the younger students of how young men must conform to the rules that were originally put into place for children lacking in discipline! Do you promise this?"

"Yes, we promise!" the youths cried, and tears shone in Szegő's eyes, but he didn't dare dry them, as he recalled that his handkerchief was dirty.

"Then shake my hand on your promise and let us part from one another as men who possess a mutual understanding, and not as people who are mortal enemies."

The boys stepped up to the headmaster one after the other and shook his hand. Laci Veres also stood in the line, but did not extend his hand. He simply passed along with the others without attracting notice. The headmaster realized it too late, his eyes flashed daggers, but he forced down his Adam's apple, then coughed it back up, ultimately resigning himself to letting him go.

"My friend," Mácsik said once they were outside. "The headman spoke well! That was manly."

"Yes," Kardos muttered. "I appreciated that."

"Hey, but he's lucky," Pista Víg said simply. "If he'd punished us, God knows we would've beaten him after our exams to the point where not one of his bones would've survived in one piece." He punctuated his words with a few obscenities.

Hounddog suddenly ran up the stairs and everyone fell silent. He flashed a hostile look through his glasses across the group. He saw that he'd arrived too late, as they'd already been excused. His eyes found Laci Veres among the others and he called out to him:

"Come now, come back. Just come, my friend!"

The boys looked after them in confusion and made their way down the stairs, whispering to one another.

"Him I will slug, I won't be kept from that!" Pista Víg said with a stifled voice, balling his large fists.

The professor rushed like a tempest into the headmaster's office.

"Excuse me," he said to the headmaster. "This can't be tolerated! This one student cannot be pardonned. If you please, this boy, this lowlife, just this past night! Last night! He was there!"

The headmaster made a grim and dour face. "Oh, please, leave me in peace! In any case the newspapers will be plastered full with that other episode. I don't want to have a scandal in the school precisely when we already have an adultery drama circulating in the town! That's why I'm the headmaster here, so that I can keep such matters quiet."

"True, true," the professors standing there said in approval.

Hounddog turned around angrily and opened the door. He went into the outer office, planted himself in front of Laci Veres, puffing himself up like a turkey.

"So, my little friend, you are escaping unscathed. Brazen hooligan. Aren't you ashamed of yourself, have you no sense of decency? Will you dare return to the home of your uncle? Enter into the presence of your honorable aunt! Shame on you! Scum. Filthy creature. That such people should walk the earth. Poisoning the air wherever they go."

He removed his glasses, looked through them, found them smeared. He removed his handkerchief and wiped them off.

"A man just educates, preaches, struggles, wrecks himself for the sake of others' children, and then such sleazy characters come along and destroy the results of their pedagogy!"

XIII

The teacher Mr. Veres busied himself in the front room and felt quite bored. He would have loved to find some excuse for going out.

"This woman has grown very old," he said to himself, observing his wife with a squint. "A man marries a young girl so that, as long as he lives, he always has a fresh, young thing around him, and this is the result."

The lady had finished dressing and was tidying up the room wearily, sloppily, like an invalid, only doing what was absolutely necessary. The maid came in and out and asked what she should do regarding the cooking.

"What do I care! Whatever you like!" the lady finally said with impatience.

The man raised his eyebrows high, causing deep wrinkles to crease his low forehead.

"What a nice wife," he said to himself, "who says regarding the midday meal that the help should do whatever she likes. Just the wife I needed. I, who in my bachelor days kept house in such a way as to make every married man envious. I held such grand farewell dinners that even my Catholic colleagues all came to my home. Even though I was just a gentleman living by myself ... I had piglets, and hogs; there was even a time when I had a cow; well, the devil take all that. There's no point in regretting things now. I did myself in by marrying."

The lady sat down in an armchair and stared out the window. Her large, sad eyes no longer twinkled, but looked languidly toward the window. "In time all will take care of itself. One day will follow after the other ..."

"My dear," the husband spoke, "I'm going into town for a bit."

She nodded, as though still participating in life, but her head just moved of its own accord. Then she looked at the window and something tugged at her to throw herself out of it. She seemed to grow faint. But she was unable to move a muscle of her strengthless body.

The teacher had already donned his hat by the door; he shifted it back and forth until it sat properly on his head, took his walking stick in his hand and smoothed out his clothes, as though that would make him more presentable.

He sensed a small pang of conscience as he descended the stairs – something seemed to whisper to him that he should remain at home, his wife was sick and in need of cheering up. But in that moment he tossed the thought from his head and attempted with impatience to focus his attention on something else, something that wasn't unpleasant, some ordinary matter.

"It's Saturday," he told himself. "Tomorrow is Sunday."

He crossed the courtyard and passed through the gate with steady steps. He intended to walk up Sikátor Street to the central tavern, as that was the fastest route, but he thought twice and opted to follow the main street through town.

"Ah, good day to you, Mr. Klein!" he greeted the carter cheerfully. Corpulent, red-faced Klein returned the greeting energetically.

"How do you do, teacher sir, how do you do! Forgive me, I didn't congratulated you yet on being named headmaster! Congratulations for you."

The teacher looked at him strangely, the improper grammar offended his ear, but the friendly attention pleased him nonetheless.

"Thank you. How have you been, Mr. Klein?"

"Not well, business is bad ... Naturally the gentlemen have it good, haha, they just chase each other through the window. Like a mob, you know, all they need is a woman and then they make chase."

"What's this, what's this? Someone was chased through a window?"

"Ah, where are you living, headmaster sir? I mean, everyone's talking about it. That young assistant judge who was just here in town. Handsome, tall, elegant young man ..."

"The deputy judge!" the teacher said, shocked.

"Yes, so the notary goes home at night and, if you please, catches his wife with the deputy judge. And, if you please, that stupid young man goes and jumps out the window and, if you please, there's a woodpile there, with stakes sticking up, and he lands there such that he ends up getting carted off to the hospital. Just like he was, in his knickers."

The teacher's mouth moved, but without emitting a sound. He merely blinked his eyes. Then he shook Klein's hand and was hastily on his way, as though he must rush off somewhere.

After a few steps he calmed down. By the time he reached the third house, he'd resigned himself to the inevitable.

The mayor was coming towards him. He greeted him.

"Good day, teacher sir," the mayor said, extending his hand.

"Good day to you, mayor sir."

The old man stood there nonchalantly, breathing asthmatically, then spoke in the local Ilosva dialect: "Once again we've got scandal to deal with, nothing but scandal. They bring all kinds of young people to the place who end up involving themselves in a lot of tomfoolery and ruin the town's good reputation."

"If you please," the teacher said, raising his eyebrows importantly from beneath his stiff black hat and blinking feverishly with his little black eyes, "if you please, yesterday that young man was at my home the entire afternoon, he conducted himself like a very solid person, I would say very respectably. We ate lunch, drank a bit of wine, absolutely nothing objectionable transpired. My wife was also quite satisfied with him. He showed himself an eminently proper gentleman. But if you please, in the evening, when he left, it could have been about nine o'clock, if you please, I noticed him looking somewhat disturbed. I could even say strange."

"Aha, aha."

"Yes, for that very reason I accompanied him. And if you please, I went with him to the doctor's house, of course! the one next to the notary's house! He wouldn't allow me to accompany him all the way! He stood there, shook my hand, and said: 'Good night, sir.'"

"Aha."

"If you please, when I went home, I wanted to tell my wife: 'You know, this man has got some evil idea into his head. He acts exactly as if he were planning on breaking and entering somewhere ...'"

"Aha."

"And did he die?"

"No, he didn't die!"

"No?" the teacher said, fearing he'd now set some unpleasant gossip in motion that could come back to haunt him down the road.

"That's the problem," the mayor reiterated, "they bring all kinds of young people here into the government offices, the public schools – something must be done about that. We've got any number of upstanding sons who were born here in town and they have to toil away in distant provinces without secure positions, and the minster just blithely sends all kinds of characters here as a form of punishment. If those people commit some mischief, then, if I may, the papers come and compromise the entire town."

He shook the teacher's hand and went off. Veres wrinkled his forehead: "Why do I keep saying 'if you please' to such as him! What an ass I am! ... Ah, Mr. Mayor, we are not reconciled because of that! Ah, if you please, a man is not broken that easily ..."

The tobacconist's wife was standing outside the door on the other side of the street and gestured toward the teacher. Veres crossed over to her.

"Oh my, teacher sir, tell me please, what was that, my God!" the tobacconist's wife said, clapping her hands together.

"He was at my home during the evening, it could have been nine o'clock when he left, but I can tell you, there was nothing wrong with him ..."

He recounted this and that, telling her everything that had happened the previous afternoon, and only then did it occur to him to ask how the misfortune had happened.

All of a sudden he was the focal point of the town, its most interesting person. The barber crossed over from the opposite side with appropriate deference to listen to their conversation ... a bootmaker likewise stood beside them, having come from the end of the street in his leather apron – he was a respected member of the presbyterate, therefore his curiosity could not be objected to. From afar, the teacher Pista Máté's form appeared, at this point in time he was in his hunting suit, his gun across his shoulder, and he yelled from the opposite side to Veres that he should come join him.

The teacher took his leave from the group, who stood assembled there together a bit longer until they'd all made the necessary observations, whereupon the tobacconist's wife went inside the tobacco shop, the barber returned to his place of work, leaving only the bootmaker, who stood there the longest; this prompted the barber to remark that, once a bootmarker has planted himself somewhere, it would require a buffalo to budge him from his spot.

"Well, old man, I hear that unlucky dog was at your place yesterday," Pista Máté said.

"Yes, yesterday from lunchtime until nine he was there."

"I've just come from Druhonyec, it's unheard of what's going on in this town. So what will happen now, what about the wife?"

"I've no idea, my friend, none whatsoever."

"Oh well, let's go inside for a glass of beer, we'll soon find out everything in there."

The little town was quiet. The sun shone hotly on the streets, but the two men who were walking along in the quantities of dust and saw that several people were standing about in front of the town hall remarked to each other breathlessly: "What a revolution. My friend, the entire town has been turned on its head!"

There were already a lot of people in the restaurant. And everyone looked inquisitively at the teacher, Veres, doubtless because everyone knew by now that the deputy judge had been at his home yesterday afternoon.

"Hm, hm," Piste Máté muttered. "The day before yesterday in the afternoon he was sitting yet in that very corner. Right, Mr. Kovács? He always sat there, in that corner!"

"Well, he won't be sitting anymore."

"Nooo?"

"He died!"

"Died!?" Máté cried. Pál Veres's mouth fell open just as it had when he'd gotten the first piece of news from the carter.

Then he sat down without uttering a word, only coming to himself when Berta brought the beer. He lifted his glass and emptied it. The cold beer made him feel better.

"That's life," he said. "Poor boy. If he'd listened to me, he'd still be alive, nothing bad would ever have happened. I told him during the evening when he wanted to leave: 'Judge, sir, don't go. Let's have a few nice drinks together, quietly, just between us, like good friends.' Then he said: 'There's something I have to do!' He said, I remember it word for word, 'there's something I have to do!' 'At nine in the evening?' I said. Because, right? he left at nine o'clock, I remember perfectly. 'At nine in the evening?' 'I already agreed to go yesterday!'"

"Ah, ah," everyone gasped.

"'I already agreed to go yesterday!' That's what he said! So please, he'd already promised to go somewhere yesterday, that is the day before yesterday! ..."

"That's good to know! That's important!" said a balding man with red-blond hair, lifting his half-empty beer glass. Veres's glass was completely empty, so before he continued his story, he waited until the girl, Berta, filled it up again, since she was already there in the room.

"That's important, indeed," the second gentleman pursued, "because it overturns the wife's statement: the notary himself said that he *wasn't expecting him*, he had no idea the deputy judge was coming there, and that the young man came there in a very agitated state!!! If I may, if he went there in such agitation, then the reason for that is that he'd been planning on something!"

"I didn't want to let him go there," Veres continued after the beer, "I also said to him: 'Judge sir, there's no need to be so mule-headed!' I said to him that he didn't have to be that mule-headed. My nephew can confirm that, he was there too."

Silence reigned for a bit.

"Such is man's fate," said a heavy-set man, the orphanage director. "One never knows when one will die. In my office we work with nothing but shocking cases of death. Here it's fortunate that no children were left behind on either side."

"What do you mean on either side? The wife didn't die."

"Sure, but she could still die. Every one of us is mortal," the orphanage director said mysteriously. But then he no longer wanted to keep the secret; he added, sighing and nodding his head: "Her husband killed her."

"The old fool," said Pista Máté, "imagine, my friend, he wasn't even a human being anymore! Not even a man. Once when we were hunting he confessed that he hadn't touched a woman in three years."

"And yet he was quite the ladies' man back in the day!" the red-haired gentleman said with a laugh.

"So what happened with your nephew?" a dark-haired man with glasses asked Veres.

"They acquitted him."

"What was the matter with him?" Máté interjected.

"Nothing," Veres said dismissively, and as he looked on the inquisitive smile that lit his colleague Bardócz's face, he thought first and foremost of what the gentleman had meant with the word "odd" that evening two days ago, and then of what might in fact have transpired that night! ... He bit his lip and stared dumbly before him.

The balding gentleman with the red-blond hair laughed out loud. "In truth, every sensation lasts only until a bigger one comes along. The little fish is eaten by the big fish, the small scandal by the big one. The entire matter was a petty student prank. No one even thinks about it any more. The professors were curious concerning the poor boy's night out. Hounddog searched up and down the entire town, asking where Laci Veres was in the night from two until three o'clock."

They burst out laughing.

"What in heaven's name!" Pista Máté shrieked, striking his fist against his forehead, then slamming it down on the table. "The devil take this Hounddog, the old man's a good friend of mine, but in my student days I also had a good deal of trouble with him. So is he still that indiscreet yet today?" and he shook his friend by the shoulder. "You know, your nephew will certainly become a somebody one day, if no one can find out where he was at night between two and three o'clock!"

Veres gaped at him and said to himself: *Where was my wife between two and three o'clock!*

"Hey! Have you gone gaga, old man?"

The teacher cringed and attempted to flash a natural smile.

In that moment the door to the corridor opened and Veres was astonished to see his day maid enter through there. Her face was stricken with horror and it was clear that she was looking for her employer, but didn't see him at first, as he was sitting in shadow.

"What's the matter, auntie?" Veres called out to her.

"Oh my, gracious sir, the gracious little lady has jumped out the window."

Everyone sprang to their feet, only Pál Veres remained sitting.

"Madame Kalafszky was by to tell about the misfortune that happened in the night over at the notary gentleman's place. And then the gracious lady just jumped out the window."

The teacher Veres gazed with a vacant stare and his lower lip hung limply.

"I ran for *pan doktor*, and madame Kalafszky spritzed water on the gracious lady. And when the doctor came, Sir Miracle Doctor told us there was nothing to worry about, as the gracious little lady would be fine, she fell in a very lucky way, like when she – with respect, sir," and she dabbed at her nose with the corner of her kerchief, "would have fallen on her ass."

Someone laughed out loud.

Pál Veres looked over, then rose to his feet, everyone laughed and he, too, managed a smile.

"Well then, thank God ... My check please, young lady ... No sooner does a man set foot outside his home than something bad happens there."

"Certainly two deaths is enough for one day," said the orphanage director. "Even though here, too, no children are involved."

"The poor lady," Máté said in a tuneful voice, "what was she thinking! What a heavenly blessing that nothing bad happened to her! The deputy judge's situation must have hit her quite hard ..."

Pál Veres was still standing there. He found it difficult to leave. He was preoccupied.

"Well, as long as nothing bad happened to my wife, I'm not concerned about the rest ... that is to say ... It's unfortunate about the young man," and he lifted his hat and took his leave. "Upon my soul, I don't even know his name. Nor does he know my own. He kept referring to me as Mr. Bovary, even though I told him several times that I'm Pál Veres. And that's a big difference! ..."

ABOUT THE TRANSLATOR

Virginia L. Lewis earned her doctorate in Modern German Literature in 1989 from the University of Pennsylvania and has studied various languages including French, Bulgarian, and of course Hungarian. She has written numerous articles on the literature of Germany, Austria, Switzerland, Romania, and Hungary. Her first translation of a novel by Zsigmond Móricz appeared with Library Cat Publishing in 2014 as *Gold in the Mud: A Hungarian Peasant Novel*. Dr. Lewis currently serves as Professor of German at Northern State University in Aberdeen, South Dakota.

Made in the USA
Columbia, SC
24 February 2020